# THE SONG
# OF
# THE MOUNTAIN

A story about two Puerta Rican teenagers
who are entrusted with the legacy
of continuing the work
of their grandmother,
a healer and a medicine woman.

This is a work of fiction. Similarities to real people, places, or events are entirely coincidental.

THE SONG OF THE MOUNTAIN

**First edition. December 2, 2024.**

Copyright © 2024 VINCENT GILVARRY.

ISBN: 979-8230359319

Written by VINCENT GILVARRY.

# Also by VINCENT GILVARRY

**Merlin's School for Aspiring Lightworkers**
Destiny Calls

**Merlin's School of Magic and Mystery**
The Thrill of The Unknown

**Standalone**
I Will Be Praying For Your Soul
Masterminds of Mischief
Fun and Games at The Passionfruit Hotel
Merlin's School of Magic and Mystery
Frozen in Time
The Miracle Man
The Song of The Mountain

Watch for more at https://vgilvarry.blog/.

# Table of Contents

# VINCENT GILVARRY

# PART ONE

# CHAPTER 1

A Life Changing Experience

It is 1955 on the island of Puerto Rico in the Caribbean, a place where the pages of history are not just tangible, they whisper tales of the past. The beating heart of the island is San Juan, a city of contrasts, but every morning and every evening without fail, the sky is transformed into a tapestry of heavenly colours.

Colonial buildings line the streets, their walls painted in shades of coral, ochre, and turquoise. Wooden shutters are thrown open to catch a salty Atlantic breeze. Laundry lines stretch between balconies and sag under the weight of drying clothes.

The streets are a symphony to daily life, where women lean out of windows and exchange gossip as they scrub floors or fold linen. The sound of a distant guitar floats through the air as does the rhythmic clip clop of hooves. And noisy little children scurry around carts that sell bacalaítos, salted codfish fritters, sweet guava pastries, and roasted sweet corn.

Men with sun-worn faces push wheelbarrows of fresh coconuts and plantains, their voices reverberating with practiced rhythm. This is a neighbourhood defined by resilience, a patchwork of people doing whatever they can to scrape by in the shadow of economic hardship.

Old San Juan is a labyrinth of narrow alleys where the cobblestone streets are damp from an early morning shower and the walls of the houses are cracked and weatherworn. Here, the air smells of fried plantains, and the aroma of bitter coffee wafts from the carts of street vendors.

San Juan is vibrant, loud, crowded, and alive and it is also the home of two teenagers, Pablo and Luna. Fifteen year old Pablo is tall for his age, and races barefoot through the alleyway, chasing a ball made from tightly bound rags. His sister Luna, two years younger and far more cautious sits on the stoop of their modest home, braiding her hair as she watches her brother with a mixture of exasperation and envy.

"Pablo, cuidado, be careful," she says, her voice carrying over the chatter of neighbours. "You are going to knock over Doña Rosa's plants again."

"Let him play," her mother Elena says with a weary smile as she takes a seat beside her daughter, her hands still covered in flour from preparing the bread for their evening meal.

"He will have to follow the rules soon enough."

Their father, Roberto, is still at work hauling heavy crates at the docks, a gruelling task which puts food on the table but only barely. The Great Depression struck Puerto Rico hard, and families are still doing their best to survive. Jobs are scarce and opportunities to escape the cycle of poverty even scarcer. Yet Elena and Roberto work tirelessly, determined to carve out a better future for their children.

It's not often that they get to spend time together, but when Roberto gets home from work he has a surprise. They are going to spend a few hours in the countryside. It's a chance to breathe fresh air and escape the relentless grind of the city, if only for a while.

As they wander along the street, Pablo races ahead, his knees scuffed from an earlier mishap, while Luna walks beside her mother carrying a bundle of fresh guavas.

"Pablo, wait," she says, her voice tinged with annoyance and affection. "He doesn't listen. He never does."

The air is heavy with the salt of the sea, and the promise of an afternoon storm hangs low in the clouds. The family make their way through a lively crowd, their laughter mingling with the rhythm of a bustling marketplace.

Luna races up to Pablo and grabs his sleeve. "You are going to get into trouble," she says.

"Not me," he says, his grin mischievous. He takes off again, and weaves through the vendors like a sparrow darting through the branches of a tree.

"Pablo, enough. Get back here now," his father cries, his voice stern.

Pablo waits for them to catch up and stays close to Luna as they cross a cobblestoned street. A horse-drawn cart trundles by and the driver offers a friendly wave.

"We should hurry. It's going to rain soon," Luna says as she glances up at the clouds.

Her mother smiles. "I think we will beat that storm before we get home."

Roberto has arranged to borrow a horse-drawn cart from a friend, and they pile in with Luna sitting between her parents. As they head off, she is chattering about the wildflowers that she wants to pick, while Pablo, perched on the edge of the cart looks ahead with eyes that speak of adventure.

The family freezes when they hear someone shouting frantically from a side street, only to be followed by the sound of pounding hooves. Pablo turns just in time to see a runaway cart heading down the hill and coming directly for them. It is full to overflowing with a cargo of heavy sacks, and as it get closer, the bags dislodge and the driver loses control.

"Jump" their father cries, but it's too late.

The accident happens suddenly and violently, the impact is deafening, the world turns inside out, accompanied by screams as the two carts collide and splinter.

And for a long time after, there is silence, and when it's over, Pablo and Luna are pulled from the wreckage by intruders but their parents were not so fortunate.

Luna wakes up a few minutes later, her ears still ringing and her knees red raw. She turns to find Pablo beside her, his face pale, his hands trembling as he gazes in disbelief at the wreckage sprawled across the street.

People come from everywhere, their faces full of shock and pity. An old woman with weathered hands kneels beside Luna, whispering words she cannot hear. Pablo gets to his feet, and heads for the wreckage, only to be pulled back by a strong armed man.

"Papá, mama," he howls. "They've gone.

Luna latches onto his arm, tears streaming down her face but Pablo doesn't cry, he just stares vacantly at the bodies of his parents, his fists clenched, his jaw trembling.

The dark clouds gathered above finally break and the rain pours down in torrents, washing the blood from the cobblestones but it's not enough to wash the shock and horror from their hearts.

In the days that follow, their once lively street is unnaturally quiet. Pablo and Luna are grief stricken and carry a burden that is far too heavy for their little shoulders. Before and after the funeral, neighbours keep a close eye on them at all times. People they have known all of their lives drop by with plates of food and broken hearts, but no one can fill the void left by the loss of their parents.

A few days later, a letter arrives, delivered by an elderly man who speaks in a voice that's almost as old as the mountains. He says that it's from their grandmother, Juana María who has offered to take them in. This is a woman the children have never met, but they have heard stories about their elderly grandmother who lives up in the mountains.

Pablo's hands are trembling as he takes the letter and just gazes at it. Luna looks to her brother, her eyes wide with fear. They will have to leave San Juan, the only home they have ever known, neither of them aware that this is the beginning of a journey that will change their lives forever.

# CHAPTER 2

The Journey into the Mountains

The following day, with hearts red raw, they say goodbye to friends and neighbours. The old man, who has been waiting patiently for several days, helps them onto his cart, and an hour later, they are winding their way through the hills of the Puerto Rican countryside

Pablo and Luna sit side by side on a worn wooden bench, their belongings reduced to a single battered suitcase at their feet. Pablo holds the makeshift ball in his hands while Luna holds a dolly made of cotton cloth. At her feet is the bag of guavas which somehow survived unscathed from the accident, a far too tender reminder of the last day they spent with their parents.

She watches vacantly as the scene changes to green fields and dense forest, but her pounding heart is a reminder that they are leaving behind everything they have ever known.

They are heading for the El Yunque rainforest and the ride up the mountain is mostly slow and silent except for the rhythmic groans and creaks of the donkey cart.

Pablo is restless, his legs shaking anxiously, but there is nothing he can do other than watch as a new and unfamiliar world starts to take shape.

"How much longer?" he says, his voice tight with impatience.

Luna doesn't know and doesn't answer. All she can think about are the words of her grandmother, *I will care for them. Send them to me at once.*

Luna can only guess what Juana María is like. She is hoping that she is not a stern figure in dark clothes, her eyes sharp and watchful. They met many years ago when Juana María made a brief visit to San Juan. Their mother rarely spoke about her, and when she did, she did so sparingly, her voice tinged with reverence and unease.

PABLO IS STILL SCOWLING but Luna barely even notices, her mind is spinning with questions. What will their lives be like now? Will they like living in the mountains, and will they like living with their grandmother?

The road disappears as the donkey cart makes its way through a forest on a journey that never seems to end. The track winds through towering trees and dense underbrush. The air is thick with the scent of rain and moss, and other than the birds singing in the trees, the only sound is the steady beat of the donkey's hooves as it hauls the cart along the road.

It is almost sunset when they finally reach Juana María's home, and Luna catches her breath. It's a small wooden house nestled in a clearing, its walls weathered and covered in creeping vines. Strange symbols are etched into the doorframe, and bundles of dried herbs hang from the eaves. A faint trail of smoke rises from the chimney, carrying with it an earthy, unfamiliar smell.

Juana María appears and her dress is homespun and simple, her hair streaked with grey, and in her hands, she holds a cane carved with an intricate pattern. Her piercing eyes sweep over the children as they approach. Pablo clutches onto Luna's arm, and for the first time since the accident his hand starts to tremble.

"You have grown," Juana María says, her voice low and firm. She studies them closely, her gaze lingering on Pablo's defiant stare and Luna's tear-streaked face.

"Come," she says. "There is no need to be afraid. After all, I am your grandmother."

Luna glances at Pablo who just wants to go back home. "Let's go."

"Why is it so quiet?" Pablo says.

"The mountain doesn't speak to intruders," Juana María says.

That cryptic remark hangs in the air and sends a shiver down his spine. He looks around at the trees, their branches like skeletal hands reaching for the sky. The weight of the mountain settles on his shoulders, heavy and watchful, and the further they travelled, the darker the forest grew, as though the sun itself refused to intrude.

"This is your home now," Juana María says.

Pablo frowns, he has unspoken questions. Luna feels his unease but forces a smile.

"Thank you, abuela."

Juana María's expression softens for a moment, a flicker of something unspoken passing through her eyes. She opens the door and says, "Come inside. There is much to learn."

As they step into the dim, herb-scented interior of the house, Luna wonders if their grandmother took them in out of love or for some other reason.

# CHAPTER 3

The Medicine Woman

The house smells of earth and fire, a strange mixture of herbs and smoke that clings to the air like a second skin. Luna hesitates in the doorway as her eyes adjust to the light. The walls are lined with shelves and jars that contain mysterious powders, roots, and dried flowers. Bundles of herbs dangle from the beams overhead, their shadows casting eerie patterns on the wooden floor.

Pablo's curiosity outweighs his caution. "What is all of this?" he says. He is not just referring to a particularly pungent aroma.

Juana María, who is stoking the fire in the hearth, turns slowly, her sharp eyes settling on each of them in turn. "This is my work," she says, her voice steady and deliberate. "And now, it's yours too."

Luna exchanges a glance with Pablo, who frowns. "We didn't ask for this," he says under his breath.

Juana María's expression hardens, and she crosses the room with surprising swiftness, her cane tapping against the floor. "No," she says as she stands before them. "But the mountain has asked. And the mountain does not wait for permission."

"The mountain?" Pablo scoffed. "It's just trees and rocks."

Juana María's gaze bears down on him, and for a moment, the room seem to grow heavier. The light from the crackling fire reflects on her stern face. "You are young," she says, her voice low. "You do not yet understand. But you will."

"What do you mean?" Luna says, her voice barely above a whisper.

Juana María gestures to a table at the back of the room, on which sit is a mortar and pestle, dried herbs, and faded books with cracked spines. She picks up a small vial filled with a pale green liquid and holds it up to the light.

"This," she says, "can heal a fever that grips a man when the forest sickness takes hold. This," she says as she gestures to a cluster of dark, twisted roots, "can draw poison from a wound. And this," she says pointing to a jar filled with what looks like soil, "can call back the spirit of a dying animal, if you know how to ask."

Luna's mind is equal parts awe and unease. Pablo folds his arms across his chest, his scepticism clearly visible. "It's just plants and dirt," he says. "Anyone can do that."

Juana María lets out a sharp, humourless laugh. "Is that what you think, that these are just plants and dirt?" She leans closer, her eyes glittering like embers. "The mountain is alive, Pablo. It breathes. It listens. It remembers. And it gives its gifts only to those who respect its power."

Pablo is about to respond but Luna grabs his arm to silence him. "Why are you telling us this, abuela?" she says.

Juana María's gaze softens for a moment. "Because my time grows short," she says, her voice quieter now. "And when I am gone, the mountain will call to you, and it will not ask if you are ready."

Luna's breath catches in her throat and notices her grandmother's weathered hands, and the faint tremor of her fingers as she places the vial back on the table. The strength that has seen Juana María through years of solitude and service is fading.

"I don't know if we can do this," Luna says, her voice trembling.

"You will learn," Juana María says. "You must."

The conversation is interrupted by a sudden, knock at the door. Juana María stiffens, her eyes narrowing. She turns to the children, her voice urgent. "Stay here."

Without waiting for a response, she opens the door and speaks to the person on the other side. Luna can't see who it is but catches fragments of the conversation. It's something about a sick child and a fever that won't break.

Juana María nods, takes a leather satchel from the table, and disappears into the night, the door creaking shut behind her.

"Where is she going?" Pablo says, his voice hushed but tense.

"To help," Luna says, her chest tight with an unfamiliar mix of fear and admiration. Their grandmother is more than a healer; she is a guardian, a bridge between the mountain and the people who depend on it for their livelihood. And now, that responsibility is inching closer to them.

The fire crackles softly, its light playing against the jars and herbs in the room. Luna turns to Pablo, her voice low. "Maybe those things are not just plants and dirt."

Pablo doesn't reply, and for the first time, he looks unsure.

# CHAPTER 4

### Ghosts of the Past

The morning fog clings to the mountain like a veil, muffling sound and sight. Juana María rises and leaves early with a satchel of herbs.

The house feels like a tomb. Luna and Pablo sit at the kitchen table picking at bowls of a thick cornmeal porridge. Pablo taps his spoon against the edge of his bowl, the rhythmic clink breaking the silence.

"Stop it," Luna says, as she pushes her half-eaten meal away.

"I'm bored," Pablo says. He glances at the shelves that line the walls, his curiosity warring with caution. The jars of dried herbs and strange powders seem to beckon.

"Why does she have so much stuff? Do you think it's magic?"

Luna frowns, unsure. The word *magic* feels dangerous, almost forbidden. "It's just her work," she says, and even as the words leave her mouth, they feel right.

Pablo isn't convinced. He stands abruptly, and scrapes the chair across the floor. "I am going to take a look around."

"Pablo, don't," Luna cries, but her brother moves to a large wooden chest that sits beneath the window, its lid carved with swirling patterns that almost look alive.

Pablo runs his fingers over the intricate designs. "What do you think is in here?"

"Leave it alone," Luna says, her voice sharp. "She'll be furious."

"She's not here," Pablo counters, a mischievous grin spreading across his face. He presses his ear to the chest, as if expecting it to whisper its secrets. When it doesn't, he releases the iron latch and lifts the lid.

The hinges groans, loud and jarring in the stillness. Luna holds her breath, her pulse quickening. The chest is filled with faded photographs, yellowed letters tied with twine, and small objects that gleam in the dim light.

Pablo pulls out a photograph, his brow furrowing as he studies it. "Hey, look at this."

The photo is old, its edges frayed and curling. It shows a younger Juana María standing beside a man and a child. The man's face is solemn, his eyes shaded, while the child, barely more than a toddler clings to his leg. Luna looks closely and realises that child is their mother.

"That's Mamá?" she says, her voice trembling.

"It has to be," Pablo says as he rummages through the chest, and pulls out more photos and letters. One letter falls from the bundle, the faded ink curling across the page in a script that is both beautiful and difficult to read.

Luna picks it up, her fingers trembling. The words are written in Spanish, but some of the phrases stand out: *la promesa del espíritu del monte—the promise of the mountain's spirit.*

"What does that mean?" Pablo says.

"I don't know," but the words send a shiver down Luna's spine. The contents of the chest include a small, polished stone, a weathered book bound in leather, and a delicate necklace strung with beads made of bone. Each item feels heavy with meaning, like pieces of a puzzle they aren't meant to solve.

"We shouldn't be doing this," Luna says, standing abruptly. "Put it back."

"Why?" Pablo says. "She's hiding things from us. What if this is why she brought us here?"

"I don't care," Luna cries, her voice louder than she intended. "She will know that we touched it."

Pablo hesitates and sighs and puts everything back into the chest. Luna hands are shaking as she places the letter back into the bundle. And just as he closes the lid, the door opens.

Juana María stands in the doorway, her sharp eyes narrowing as they take in the scene. For a moment, she says nothing, but the weight of her gaze is almost suffocating.

"What are you doing?" she says, with a distinctive tone to her voice

Pablo freezes and Luna steps forward, her heart pounding. "We were just looking."

"Looking where you shouldn't," Juana María says, her tone cold. She crosses the room, her cane tapping against the floor with measured precision. She stops in front of the chest and places her hand on the lid as if to reassure herself that it's intact.

"These are not toys," she says, her voice soft but firm. "They are memories. And they are not for you."

Luna's cheeks burn with shame. "I'm sorry."

Juana María looks at her for a long moment. "Sorry will do for now but understand this, both of you." Her eyes darken, her voice like the rumble of distant thunder. "The mountain does not forgive curiosity. If you meddle where you do not belong, it will make you pay."

Pablo swallows hard; his bravado gone. Luna is all too aware of the weight of her grandmother's words.

Juana María straightens up. "Now, go outside and gather some water from the spring. And tonight, we will speak of what you *can* know."

Their hearts are racing and as they follow the path to the spring, Luna glances back at the house, its shadow looming against the trees.

"What do you think she meant?" Pablo says.

"I don't know," Luna replies. But deep down, she does know.

# CHAPTER 5

The First Lesson

The air inside Juana María's house is heavy with the scent of burning sage. A thin wisp of smoke rises up from a small clay dish on the table where their grandmother had placed a smouldering bundle of dried leaves.

Luna and Pablo sat stiffly at the table, their backs straight, their hands resting awkwardly in their laps. In the flickering light, shadows dance on the walls, and the symbols etched into the beams move like shifting spectres.

Juana María stands before them, her cane resting against the table, her hands deftly grinding dried herbs in a mortar. "The mountain provides all things," she says, her voice even and deliberate. "For those who know how to listen."

Pablo's brow furrows. "Listen to what? Trees don't talk."

With a clearly defined look, Juana María silences his protest. "The mountain speaks in whispers. In the rustle of leaves, the rush of water, the call of the coquí at dusk. You cannot hear it because you are not paying attention."

Luna leans forward, her heart thudding in her chest. There is something in her grandmother's voice, an urgency, a weight that she understands even if the words feel strange and distant.

Juana María picks up a bundle of dried flowers, their petals shrivelled and brown. "This is *anamu* which is also known as garlic weed" she says, as she holds it out for them to see. "It smells bitter but its power is strong. It draws out sickness and calms fevers."

She place the flowers in a clay bowl and drenches them with boiling water, and a pungent, earthy aroma fills the room. "You will learn to recognize these plants, to know their voices. Each one is a gift from the mountain."

"It smells like wet dirt," Pablo says.

Juana María arches an eyebrow, a faint smile tugging at the corner of her lips. "And yet, wet dirt will save your life one day, my boy. Do not mock what you do not understand."

Luna nudges Pablo with her elbow, silently willing him to be quiet. Their grandmother's gaze turns to her, softer now.

"Come here, Luna."

She slides off the chair and approaches the table. Juana María places a mortar and pestle in her hands, heavy with the weight of stone.

"Crush these," Juana María says, as she adds a handful of dried leaves to the mortar. "Slowly. Let the leaves speak to you."

Luna glances up, unsure if this is a test or a lesson, but Juana María's face gives nothing away. She starts to grind the leaves, the brittle edges crumbling under the pestle. A faint, sharp aroma arises from the mixture and makes her eyes water.

"Good," Juana María says. "Now tell me, what do you feel?"

Luna pauses, confused. "I don't feel anything."

Juana María places a weathered hand over hers, guiding the pestle in slow, deliberate circles. "You are thinking too much. Close your eyes and feel."

Luna hesitates and then obeys. The rough texture of the leaves under the stone, the subtle resistance of the herbs as they break down, the faint vibrations in her fingertips, and then, her breathing slows.

"Now you are listening," Juana María says softly, as she withdraws her hand. "The mountain speaks in sensations, not words. Always pay attention."

Pablo watches, his frown deepening. "What about me?"

Juana María turns to him, her sharp gaze making an assessment. She picks up a small vial filled with dark liquid and places it in his hands. "This is for burns. Take it to the fire and warm it gently."

"Why do I have the easy part?"

Juana María chuckles, a dry sound like the rustling of leaves. "There is no easy part, *muchacho*. If you warm it too quickly, it will burn. If you are careless, it will spill. Do it right or you will start over."

Grumbling under his breath, Pablo carries the vial to the fire, kneels beside the hearth, his face set in concentration as he holds the vial over the flame. Luna is surprised by the care in his movements.

That was their first lesson in the preparation of medicinal plants, and when it's over, Juana María nods and smiles. "Today, you have taken your first steps. The mountain has watched, and it has judged you ready."

"Ready for what?" Pablo says, his voice wary.

"To learn," Juana María replies. "The mountain does not give its knowledge freely. It tests you at every turn. If you are careless, it will punish you. If you are greedy, it will abandon you. But if you are patient, and if you listen, it will give you everything."

Her words hang in the air, heavy and foreboding. Luna is torn between scepticism and curiosity and feels a strange sense of fear and excitement, as if she is standing on the edge of an abyss.

Juana María's hands move deftly as she tidies up the herbs and tools. "Now go," she says. "The day is not over, and there is water to fetch. Do not waste time."

Luna and Pablo head for the door and are met by the cool mountain air. As they follow the path to the spring, Pablo breaks the silence.

"Luna, she is serious about this," he says.

"I think we should be too."

The mountain is listening, the trees whisper in the breeze, and the leaves rustle as if they have secrets that are yet to be told.

# CHAPTER 6

A Test of Faith

Just as the last rays of sunlight dip behind the mountain, plunging the house into shadow, there's a knock on the door, sharp and urgent. Juana María pauses and leaves the fresh herbs on the table.

She exchanges a glance with Luna and Pablo, wipes her hands, and without a word, moves to the door.

She opens it only to find a man, his face pale and slick with sweat. "Doña Juana," he gasps, his voice tight with panic. "It's my son, he is burning hot and he won't wake up."

"How long has this been going on?" she says.

"Two days now," the man replies. "We have tried everything. Please. Come and look at him."

"Yes, I will."

She turns to Luna and Pablo, her face grim. "You will come with me," she says as she places supplies in her satchel. "It's time for you to see the work that I do."

Pablo is not so sure. "What kind of work do you mean?"

"The kind that saves lives," Juana María replies, her tone decisive. "Now, let's go."

The children step out into the night where the air smells of damp earth and rain, the moonlight casts silver streaks across the path as they follow the man deeper into the forest. Shadows loom around them and the trees whisper softly in the wind.

"Where do you live?" Luna says, her voice barely above a whisper.

"On the far ridge," the man replies. "It's not far."

The house comes into view a few minutes later, a small wooden shack with a thatched roof. Inside, the air is thick with heat and desperation. A woman kneels beside a low bed, wringing her hands as she says a frantic prayer. On the bed is a boy who is no older than six, his face flushed, his small body trembling.

Juana María sweeps into the room, her presence filling the space like a storm. She kneels beside the boy, and places a hand on his forehead, her lips pressed into a thin line.

"Fever has him in its grip," she says. "But it has not yet claimed him."

She turns to Luna and Pablo. "Bring water. Quickly."

Luna grabs a clay jug and pours the water into a bowl, then hands it to Juana María who dip a cloth into the cool liquid and places it to the boy's forehead.

"Now, listen carefully," Juana María says, her voice low but firm. "Luna, in my bag, you will find a pouch of dried *guayaba* leaves. Bring them to me. Pablo, take the mortar and grind this bark into a powder."

She removes a small strip of dark, knotted bark from her satchel and gives it to Pablo whose hands tremble as he takes it.

"What's it for?" he says, his voice tight.

"It draws the heat from within," Juana María says The weight of her words hanging heavy in the air. "But only if they are prepared correctly. Do not fail."

Luna rummages through the bag and removes a pouch with a bundles of leaves, and hands them to Juana María who crushes them between her hands only to release a sharp, tangy aroma.

Pablo works away furiously at the mortar, his small hands fumbling with the pestle. "It's not breaking down," he says, frustration creeping into his voice.

"Patience," Juana María says. "The mountain rewards patience."

Luna watches as her grandmother combines the crushed leaves with the powdered bark and mixes them into a thick paste. She adds a few drops of oil from a vial, her hands moving with practiced precision. The mixture steams faintly and releases a pungent, earthy aroma.

"Luna, hold him still," Juana María says. "This will burn, but it must be done."

Luna hesitates as she looks into the boy's flushed face. His mother's pleading, tear-streaked gaze meets hers, and Luna swallows her fear, kneels beside the boy and holds his shoulders as tightly as she can, only to find that he has a scorching hot temperature.

Juana María applies the paste to the boy's chest, her fingers moving with deliberate care. The boy whimpers, his body twitching under Luna's grip.

"What's happening?" Pablo says.

"The fever fights," Juana María says, her eyes never leaving the boy. "But it will lose."

Minutes pass and the tension in the room is thick. The boy's body begins to cool under Luna's hands, and his trembling eases into stillness. His breathing, once shallow and ragged, grows deeper.

Juana María leans back and sighs. "It is done."

The mother sobs and holds her hands to her chest. "He will live?" she cries.

"He will wake by morning," Juana María says. "But you must keep him cool and give him this tea."

"It is made from these herbs. They will not let the fever return."

The woman's gratitude spills out in hurried words. "Thank you, Doña Juana. Thank you."

As they leave the house and head off into the night, Pablo finally speaks. "How did you know it would work?"

"I didn't," Juana María says. "But I trust the mountain. And now, so must you."

Luna glances at her brother, his face pale in the moonlight. She saw the doubt and fear in his eyes, but now, there's something new, a flicker of belief.

The forest seems to hum softly, as if the mountain itself is satisfied with the outcome.

# CHAPTER 7

Secrets in the Shadows

That night is different. Luna and Pablo sit at the table watching as their grandmother writes in her worn leather book, and the only sound is that of her pencil, her brow furrowed in concentration.

Luna shifts in her chair, unable to shake the unease she has felt since the night before. The way her grandmother spoke about the mountain, and about trusting it is more than just folklore. There is something real in her words, something powerful but not frightening.

Pablo finally breaks the silence, his voice hushed but firm. "Abuela, what did you mean when you said the mountain speaks to you?"

Juana María stops writing and places the book to the side with deliberate care before turning to face them. Her sharp eyes gleam in the flickering candlelight, unreadable and piercing.

"You are ready to ask," she says, her voice low. "That's a good start."

"Ready for what?" Luna says, her throat tight.

Juana María leans back in the chair, her fingers drumming lightly on the table. "The mountain is alive," she says, her words deliberate. "It watches. It remembers. And it gives gifts to those of its choosing. But those gifts come at a cost."

"What kind of cost?" says a worried Pablo.

Juana María doesn't answer immediately. Instead, she rises from the chair and motions them to follow. "Come."

The siblings exchange a wary glance and follow her to the chest at the far corner of the room. Juana María kneels beside it, her movements slow and deliberate, and runs her fingers over the carved patterns on the lid.

"This chest holds more than memories," she says, her voice barely above a whisper. "It holds a promise."

"A promise to who?" Luna says.

"To the mountain," Juana María replies. She opens the chest, the lid creaking as it reveals the faded photographs, yellowed letters, and other objects. But this time, she doesn't linger on the pictures or the trinkets, she removes a small, dark leather book and hands it to Luna.

"Open it," she says.

The cover of the book is cool and rough and Luna's hands tremble as she opens it to the first page. Intricate drawings of plants and symbols fill the yellowed paper, and the words and letters are written in an elegant but foreign script.

"This is the Codex of the Mountain," Juana María says. "It has been passed down through our family for generations. In these pages are the secrets of the power of the mountain and the burden that comes with it."

Luna's catches her breath; each page contains drawings that are both elaborate and strange. A serpent coiled around a tree. A moon that has been split in two. Hands reach out of the earth. She looks up at her grandmother and says, "What does it mean?"

"It means that our family has been chosen," Juana María says. "We are the guardians of the mountain. We listen to its voice, and we act as its hands. We heal, we protect, and when necessary, we punish."

Pablo recoils. "Punish? What does that mean?"

Juana María's eyes darken. "There are those who would seek to harm the mountain. To take its gifts for themselves without respect or understanding. When they come, and they always come, it is our duty to stop them."

The weight of her words settle over the room like a thick fog. Luna closes the book, her heart pounding in her chest. "Why us?" she says. "Why our family?"

"Because the mountain has chosen us," Juana María says simply. "And because the choice is not ours to refuse."

Pablo shakes his head, his jaw tightening. "This is crazy. Plants and dirt can't punish people. They're just...plants."

Juana María's expression softens, though her eyes remain sharp. "You think this is about plants, boy? This is about power. And power, whether you believe in it or not, always finds a way to make itself known."

She holds up a small vial with a dark, shimmering liquid that moves around like molten gold. "This," she says, "is what happens when the mountain chooses to strike back."

Luna and Pablo stare at the vial, and the air around seems to hum with an energy they can't explain. Juana María places the vial back in the chest and closes the lid.

"You have much to learn," she says, her tone softer now. "But for tonight, you will sleep. The mountain is watching, and it is patient. It will test you when the time is right."

As the siblings return to their beds, the darkness of the room seems heavier than before. The shadows press closer, and Luna listens to the wind whispering outside. She turns to Pablo, who is staring at the ceiling, his expression troubled.

"Do you believe her?" he says quietly.

Luna hesitates, the weight of the book still lingering in her hands. "I don't know, but I don't think we have a choice."

Pablo doesn't respond. The wind grows louder, carrying with it the faint sound of leaves rustling, like a voice speaking a language neither of them can understand.

# CHAPTER 8

The Prophecy

The fire in the hearth burns low and casts flickering shadows across the room. Luna and Pablo sit on the floor, their legs crossed, their grandmother towering above them as she leans heavily on her cane.

Her face is illuminated by the warm glow of the flames, every crease and line deepened by the light. In her other hand, she holds the Codex of the Mountain, its weathered cover pulsing faintly with an energy of its own.

"You are wondering why you are here," Juana María says her voice low but steady. "Why the mountain has called you. Tonight, you will know."

Luna's hands are clenched in her lap. Pablo sits rigid beside her, his jaw tight, his scepticism barely masking the fear in his eyes.

Juana María opens the Codex, her fingers moving carefully over its pages. She stops at an illustration that spans two pages: a mountain peak crowned with swirling mist; its base entwined with thick roots that seem to stretch into the heart of the earth. In the middle of the image is a blazing sun split into two, one golden, one black.

"This is the Prophecy of the Mountain," Juana María says, as she traces the image with her gnarled finger. "It's as old as the land itself and has been passed down through generations of our family. It speaks of a time when the balance of the mountain will be threatened, when its gifts will be twisted into a curse."

"What does that have to do with us?" Pablo says, his voice sharper than he intended.

Juana María's gaze is fixed and unwavering. "Because the prophecy speaks of two children, born of this bloodline. Siblings. One who will bring harmony, and one who will bring destruction."

The room falls silent. The fire crackles softly, the sound magnified in the stillness. Luna's mind is racing to grasp the meaning of Juana María's words.

"Wait," Pablo says, shaking his head. "You're saying...it's about us?"

Juana María nods. "You are the children of the prophecy."

"That's ridiculous," Pablo says, as he rises to his feet. "We're just kids. We didn't ask for this."

"The mountain does not ask," Juana María says, her voice calm but firm. "It chooses."

"But why us?" Luna says, her voice trembling. "How can we be part of something like this?"

Juana María closes the Codex and places it on the table. She moves closer, her cane tapping softly against the wooden floor. "Because you carry the blood of the mountain in your veins."

"Your mother tried to shield you from the truth, but it cannot be denied. The mountain was watching you, even when you were far away."

Luna feels a chill run down her spine. She thinks back to the strange dreams she has had ever since arriving, dreams of roots twisting through the earth, of whispering trees, of an endless darkness calling her name. She glances at Pablo who avoids her gaze.

"And this harmony and destruction?" Pablo says, his voice tight. "What does that mean?"

"It means your choices will determine the mountain's fate," Juana María says. "One of you will protect its gifts, ensuring that its power remains a force of balance. The other may allow greed, fear, or anger to twist that power into something dangerous."

Pablo's face darkened. "So are we supposed to sit here and wait for the mountain to decide that we are good enough?"

"No," Juana María says sharply. "You must decide. The mountain only reflects what is already within your soul."

"What if we make the wrong choice?" Luna says.

Her grandmother's expression softens, a rare flicker of vulnerability passing through her eyes. "Then the mountain will suffer. And so will all who depend on it."

The weight of her words settle heavily on the children. Pablo paces the room, his hands clenched into a fist. Luna stares at the Codex, its cover seems darker now, almost ominous.

"How do we stop it?" Luna says.

"By learning. By listening. The mountain will test you. It will show you its secrets, its power, its dangers. And when the time comes, you must decide how to act."

"And if we don't?" Pablo says, his voice low.

Juana María's gaze is unyielding. "Then the balance will break. And you will have to live with what follows."

Pablo stops pacing, his shoulders tense. "This isn't fair," he says.

"No," Juana María agrees. "It is not. But life rarely is."

The fire flickers, casting long shadows that seem to be reaching out for the children. Luna's chest aches with the weight of the prophecy, the enormity of what Juana María is asking of them. She thinks about their parents, of the lives they lost and feels a pang of longing for a simpler time.

"I don't want to hurt the mountain," Luna says softly.

"Then you are already on the right path."

"And me?" Pablo says, his voice tight. "What if I mess up?"

Juana María's eyes soften and for the first time, her sternness gave way to something gentler. "We all falter, *mijo*. But it is not one choice that defines you. It is the sum of them all."

The room falls silent again, the weight of the prophecy settling over them like a heavy blanket. The fire burn lower, its light dimming as the night deepens.

Juana María turns to the door, her cane tapping softly as she moves. "Rest now," she says. "The mountain is patient, but not forever. Tomorrow, we begin the real work."

As she disappears into her bedroom, Luna and Pablo are left alone with the crackling fire and the lingering echo of her words. Luna turns to her brother, her voice trembling.

"What if she's right?" she says.

Pablo doesn't answer but stares at the Codex, his jaw tightening. "Then we don't have a choice," he says. "We just have to figure it out."

Outside, the wind howls through the trees, its voice carrying a message that only the mountain can understand.

# CHAPTER 9

Breaking Point

The morning sky is grey and oppressive and the mist clings to the mountain like a second skin. Luna stands at the edge of the clearing, her arms wrapped tight as she watches the fog swirl through the trees. The weight of the prophecy presses on her thoughts like a stone she cannot dislodge.

She can feel the quiet tension inside the house. Pablo's voice carries through the walls, sharp and frustrated as he argues with Juana María again. He has been like this all morning, and every question is met with a vague answer, and every attempt at understanding is met with another layer of mystery.

Luna's head is pounding and she can't take it anymore. The atmosphere is stifling and thick with unspoken fears and rising tempers. She needs space, a moment to breathe.

A moment later, Pablo storms out of the house, his fists clenched, his face red with frustration. "I can't do this anymore," he cries as he kick away at a few loose stones.

"She won't tell us anything real. Just riddles and stories."

"Pablo, calm down," Luna says softly, but he shakes his head.

"No, don't tell me to calm down. You heard her last night. One of us is supposed to ruin everything. What kind of game is this?"

"It's not a game," Luna says, though the words feel hollow in her mouth.

"Then what is it? It feels like we are pawns in some story she has been telling herself for decades."

Luna's gaze is fixed on the trees and she doesn't know how to answer, because part of her agrees. None of this feels fair, and the more she thinks about it, the more the questions she has. Why did the mountain choose them? How are they supposed to protect something they don't even understand?

"I don't want this," Pablo cries, his voice at breaking point. "I didn't ask for any of it."

"Neither did I," Luna says. "But it's not about what we want. It's about what's at stake."

"And what is that, exactly?" Pablo shoots back. "The mountain? The people? We don't even know what any of this really means!"

His words hit harder than she expected.

"I am trying, Pablo," she says, her voice trembling. "I am trying to understand. To listen. Why can't you?"

"Because this isn't real," he cries. "It's just stories, Luna. Stories about plants and dirt and...and magic. None of it makes sense."

"Maybe it doesn't make sense to you because you won't let it," Luna says, the anger rising in her chest.

"You're so busy being angry that you are not even trying."

"Trying to do what? Be the perfect little saviour?" Pablo says. "Maybe you're fine with all of this, but I'm not. I just want to go back to San Juan. Back to a normal life."

"Normal?" Luna cries "There's nothing left for us in San Juan, Pablo. You think running away will fix this? It won't. The mountain will follow us, just like it always has. You can't escape from it."

"Watch me," Pablo says coldly.

"You're such a coward," she cries. "All you do is complain and push everyone away. Maybe the mountain made a mistake choosing you."

Pablo's face darkens, his hands rolling into fists. "Maybe it did," he said, his voice low. "Maybe you are the one it should be worried about."

The words cut deeper than Luna expected. Her throat tightens, but she refuses to let him see her cry. She turns on her heel and heads for the forest, her heart pounding in her chest.

"Where are you going?" Pablo says.

"Anywhere but here," she replies without looking back.

The forest closes around her, its shadows cool and quiet compared to the storm that rages inside. She stumbles over roots and rocks, her breath coming in sharp gasps, and when she finally stops, she leans against a tree, her legs trembling.

She wipes the tears from her eyes. Why does Pablo have to be like this? Why can't he see what she sees, feel what she feels? The mountain isn't just trees and rocks, it is alive. She can feel it in every breath of wind, every time the leaves rustle.

She closes her eyes, trying to steady her nerves. The forest seems to hum, a low, soothing vibration that wraps around her like a blanket. Slowly, her anger begins to fade, replaced by something quieter. Sadness. Fear.

"Why us?" she whispers to the trees, her voice breaking. "What are we supposed to do?"

The forest doesn't answer, but the wind picks up, carrying with it the faint scent of flowers and earth. Luna opens her eyes and sees a beam of sunlight piercing the canopy, illuminating a small clearing ahead.

Drawn by something she can't explain, she decides to have a look. At the centre of the clearing is a single white flower, its petals glowing faintly in the light. It is delicate and beautiful but there's something powerful about it, something ancient.

Luna kneels, her fingers brushing against the petals. A strange calm washes over her, and for the first time in days, she feels like she can breathe again.

Back at the house, Pablo sits on the steps, his head in his hands. The weight of his argument with Luna has affected him more than he realises. It is heavy and suffocating, but he looks to the forest, guilt twisting in his chest.

He doesn't know if he believes in the mountain or the prophecy or any of it, but he does know one thing: he can't face it alone.

# CHAPTER 10

Juana María's Farewell

The following morning, the mountain is wrapped in a heavy mist that clings to the trees like a shroud. Luna and Pablo sit at the kitchen table, their eyes puffy from a sleepless night. Neither have spoken since the argument of the day before, the silence is thick and brittle, and ready to shatter at the slightest word.

The sound of Juana María's footsteps breaks the silence. She moves slower than usual, her cane tapping against the floor with an uneven rhythm. Her face is pale, the sharp lines of her features softened by exhaustion. A ripple of unease is evident in the room.

"Today is the day," she says, her voice quiet but firm. "The mountain has called."

"Called for what?" Pablo says, his voice tinged with irritation but lacking the bite of the night before.

Juana María fixes her sharp gaze on him. "For me."

The words hang in the air, heavy and final. "What do you mean?" Luna says, her voice trembling.

Her movements slow and deliberate, Juana María sits on the opposite side of the table. "My time has come," she says simply. "I have served the mountain, but I am only its keeper for a season. Now, it's your turn."

"No," Luna cries. "You don't mean that."

"I do," Juana María says gently. "This is how it has always been. The mountain takes as it gives. My body has grown tired, and my spirit must return to the land."

"You're just going to leave? What about us? We don't know what to do. We're not ready."

"You are ready enough," Juana María says, her voice soft but resolute. "You have questions, and you have doubts. That is how it should be. But the mountain does not wait for perfection."

Luna's mind is racing. "There has to be something we can do. Some way to stop this."

"There is nothing that can stop death," Juana María says as she places her weathered hand on Luna's. "This is not an ending, niña. It is a passing. The mountain is calling me home."

Pablo shoves his chair back abruptly, the legs scraping against the floor. "This is insane," he cries. "How can you just accept this?"

Juana María turn her gaze to him, her eyes soft but unyielding. "Because I trust the mountain. And so must you."

"I can't," he says. "I don't even know if I believe in any of this."

Juana María smiles faintly, her expression tinged with sadness. "You will. When the time comes, you will feel the mountain in your bones, in your blood. You may not believe it now, but the mountain believes in you."

Trembling, Pablo turn away. Luna is torn between wanting to comfort him and wanting to cling to their grandmother, to beg her to stay.

Juana María rises from the chair, her movements slow but steady. "Come with me," she says. "There is one last thing I must show you."

The siblings follow Juana María to a clearing they have never seen before, a place where the trees open to reveal a circle of stones, each surface etched with the same swirling patterns that adorn the Codex.

At the centre of the circle is a very old tree, its bark silver with age. Juana María kneels and places her hands on its roots. She closes her eyes, her lips moving silently, as though speaking to something only she can hear.

She gestures to Luna and Pablo to come closer. "Kneel," she says, her voice soft but commanding.

The siblings obey, and Juana María reaches into her satchel and removes two small objects wrapped in cloth and passes one to each of them.

She gives Luna a pendant carved from a dark, polished stone, and to Pablo she gives a stone with edges jagged.

"These are the talismans of the mountain," Juana María says. "They will guide you when I cannot."

"What do we do with them?" Luna says.

"Listen to them," Juana María says, her voice filled with a quiet certainty. "They will show you the way. The mountain looks after its own."

"You will make mistakes and you will stumble, but you will find your path. And when you do, the mountain will be with you."

"I don't want you to go," Luna cries.

Juana María kisses her on the forehead. "You are stronger than you know, *niña*. Trust yourself."

Pablo swallows hard, his voice tight. "What if we can't do this? What if we mess everything up?"

Juana María smiles, her eyes filled with a deep, unshakable love. "You won't. I believe in you."

She turns back to the tree, her hands pressed against the bark, and for a moment, she stands perfectly still. Then the wind picks up and swirls around the clearing, carrying with it the scent of earth and rain.

As the wind grows stronger, Juana María's figure seems to blur, the edges of her form dissolving into the air. The siblings watch in stunned silence as their grandmother fades, her voice carried away on the breeze.

"Trust the mountain," she says. "It will not lead you astray."

And then she is gone, leaving only the faint rustle of leaves and the talismans clutched in their hands.

# CHAPTER 11

A New Bond

The siblings are in a state of shock, the clearing is silent, and the air thick with the weight of what just happened. Luna kneels down, her pendant clutched tightly in her trembling hands. Her heart pounds in her chest, and her breath is shallow as she gazes at the space where Juana María stood only moments ago. The towering tree now seems older, more ancient, as if it absorbed their grandmother into its roots.

Pablo stands a few feet away, his fists clenched at his sides, his face pale and blank. He doesn't look at Luna or the tree. His eyes are fixed on the ground, his jaw tight as if he is holding back a scream.

"She's gone," Luna cries, her voice cracking.

Pablo doesn't respond. He turns away abruptly, his movements stiff as he walks back to the house. Luna scrambles to her feet. "Pablo, wait."

He doesn't stop. His shoulders are tense, his pace quick, his steps heavy. Luna hesitates for a moment, her heart torn between grief and the need to follow him.

She runs after him, the pendant bouncing against her chest with every step, and when she catches up, she grabs his arm and forces him to stop. "You can't just walk away!"

Pablo yanks his arm free and turns on her. His face is a mask of anger, his eyes are blazing. "What do you want me to do, Luna? She has gone. She left us."

"She didn't leave us," Luna says, her voice shaking. "She trusted us. She believed in us."

"Believed in *you,* maybe," Pablo snaps. "Not me. I am the one who is supposed to mess everything up, remember?"

"That is not what she said."

"It is what she meant," Pablo says. "She knew one of us was going to fail, and I know it's going to be me. So why even try?"

"Because it's not about being perfect," Luna shoots back, her voice rising. "She told us that we would make mistakes. She told us that we would stumble. That's part of it."

Pablo shakes his head, his expression bitter.

"You don't get it, do you? You are always the one who's calm, who listens, who believes. And I am angry all the time. What if that is what the mountain sees in me? What if I *am* the one who ruins everything?"

Luna stares at him, her heart aching. For all his bravado, Pablo looks like a lost child, his anger masking the fear that shines in his eyes. She takes a deep breath and steadies herself.

"We don't know what the mountain sees," she says gently. "But I know you, Pablo. You are not angry. You care. You cared about Mamá and Papá. And you care about me. That's what matters."

Pablo's shoulders sag, his bravado crumbling. "I don't know if I can do this," he says.

"You don't have to do it alone," Luna says. "We're in this together. Just like always."

Pablo looks at her, his eyes filling with unshed tears. For a moment, he says nothing and then nods. "Okay," he says, his voice barely audible. "We are in this together."

Luna smiles and reaches out to take his hand but he doesn't pull it away. They walk back to the house in silence, the mist thickening around them. The forest seems quieter than usual, as if the mountain itself is holding its breath. When they reach the clearing, the sight of Juana María's house feels oddly comforting.

Inside, the fire in the hearth has burned down to glowing embers, casting a warm light over the room. The Codex sits on the table, its leather cover gleaming faintly. Luna places her hand over above the book.

"What now?" Pablo says, his voice hesitant.

Luna looks at him and then at the Codex. She opens it to a random page, her eyes scanning the intricate drawings and unfamiliar script. "We start here," she says. "We learn."

Pablo sighs and pulls up a chair. "This is going to be hard, isn't it?"

"Probably," Luna says, "But we have been through worse."

Pablo chuckles and the tension between them eases. "Yeah. I guess we have."

They spend the rest of the evening poring over the Codex, their heads bent close as they try to make sense of its mysteries. For the first time in days, the silence between them feels less like a barrier and more like a shared understanding.

As the night deepens, the wind outside picks up, rustling the trees and carrying with it the faint, familiar scent of sage.

Luna looks up from the book, her heart steadying as she feels a strange sense of calm.

The mountain is watching. It has always been watching. And for the first time, Luna is ready to watch back.

# CHAPTER 12

The Song of the Mountain

The night air is thick and electric, the kind of silence that presses into the skin and whispers of something stirring but just out of reach. Luna wakes abruptly, her heart pounding as if she has been running. The room is dark and the faint glow of the dying fire casts long shadows on the walls.

The pendant around her neck feels strangely warm against her chest. A soft hum fills the air, so faint she thought she might have imagined it. But then it comes again, a low vibration that seems to echo in her bones.

"Pablo," she says, as she tries to wake her brother.

Pablo groans and rolls onto his side. "What now?" he mumbles, his voice thick with sleep.

"Something's happening," Luna says urgently. "The mountain, I think it's calling us."

Pablo opens one eye, his brow furrowing. "Calling? Are you serious?"

"Yes," she says. "Can you feel it?"

His hand instinctively reaches for the pendant around his neck. His expression shifts as the hum grows stronger and reverberates through the room.

"I can feel it, but what does it mean?"

"I don't know," Luna says as she grabs the Codex from the table. "But we need to find out."

They dress quickly and the hum becomes louder when they step out into the cold, moonlit night. The mist hangs low over the ground, and swirls around their ankles as they move. The sound isn't coming from the house, it's coming from the forest.

"Are we really going to do this?" Pablo says, his voice tense.

"Do you have a better idea?"

"No," he says. "But I don't like it."

The forest is alive in a way that it has never been before. The trees sway gently even though there is no wind, and the air is thick with the scent of earth and moss. The hum pulls them deeper into the woods, past familiar paths and into territory neither have been before.

The humming sound grows stronger, and changes into what sounds like a melody, a haunting, wordless song that seems to come from the very earth beneath their feet.

"What is this place?" Pablo says as they emerge into a clearing bathed in silver light.

At the centre of the clearing is an ancient stone altar, its surface covered in moss and etched with the same swirling patterns they saw in the Codex. The air around it shimmers as though the moonlight itself is bending down to touch it.

As Luna steps forward, her pendant grows warmer. Pablo follows reluctantly, his hand gripping the jagged talisman around his neck.

"What do we do?" he says, his voice barely audible.

Luna opens the Codex and flips through the pages until she finds a drawing of the altar. The text beside it is written in the same looping script she struggled to decipher before, but now the words seem to shift and blur and arrange themselves into something she can understand.

"It's a test," she says, her voice trembling. "A trial of the mountain's power."

"What kind of trial?" Pablo says, his eyes darting nervously around the clearing.

"It says we have to prove that we are worthy. That we can protect the mountain's secrets."

Pablo frowns. "And how exactly do we do that?"

Before Luna can answer, the air around them shifts and the shimmering light intensifies, and then, the ground beneath their feet trembles. A low, rumbling voice echoes through the clearing, ancient and commanding, but what they hear are not words.

The siblings exchange a wide-eyed glance, and then, as if pulled by an unseen force, they step closer to the altar.

They are enveloped by darkness, as if the moonlight has been swallowed by an inky shadow. The hum turns into a roar, and the forest around them seems to close in, the trees bending and twisting as though alive.

From the darkness, shapes emerge, phantoms of the past, their forms flickering like dying embers. A woman carrying a basket of herbs. A man kneeling by a wounded animal. A child placing stones in a circle. Each figure moves with purpose, their actions deliberate and ritualistic.

"Who are they?" Pablo says, his voice shaking.

"I think they are the guardians," Luna says, her throat tight. "The ones who came before us."

As the last phantom disappears, the ground beneath the altar splits open, only to reveal a gaping chasm. A faint golden light glows from its depths, pulsing like a heartbeat. The voice of the mountain rumbles again and the sound resonates in their chest.

Luna steps forward, her eyes locked on the chasm. "We have to trust it," she said.

"Trust *what*?" Pablo says. "It's a giant hole in the ground, Luna. We don't even know what's down there."

"Exactly," she says, as she grips her pendant. "That's the point. The mountain doesn't give answers, it asks for trust."

Pablo hesitates, his jaw tightening. "And what if it's a trap? What if we fail?"

Luna looks at him, her gaze steady. "Then we fail together."

The words hang in the air for a moment before Pablo let out a shaky breath. "Fine," he says. "Together."

As they step onto the altar, the hum drowns out everything else, it is almost deafening, and then, they are enveloped by a golden light.

For a moment, there is nothing, no sound, no sight, no sensation. Then, the light fades and they find themselves standing on a narrow ledge deep within the mountain. The air is cool and damp, the walls glistening with veins of crystal that pulse with light.

At the far end of the ledge is a small pedestal, and on it rests a smooth, black stone that seems to absorb the light around it.

"That's it," Luna says, her voice barely above a whisper. "That's what the mountain wanted us to find."

Pablo frowns. "And now what?"

Luna reaches for the stone, which is warm, almost alive, and as she holds it, a surge of energy courses through her veins. Images flash into her mind, trees, rivers, storms, and fire. And then they hear voice of the mountain again, only this time it's softer, almost tender.

"We have to take it with us," she says.

Pablo hesitates and then place his hand over hers. The stone pulses once and then falls silent, its warmth spreading until it has suffused every element of their being.

They make their way out of the chasm and return to the clearing, and the forest seems to exhale, the tension lifting like a heavy veil. The was a test and they answered.

# CHAPTER 13

Guardians of the Legacy

The first light of dawn breaks over the mountain, casting a pale golden glow through the trees. The clearing where the altar stood is now quiet, its ancient power has settled, as if the mountain itself is at peace.

As they emerge from the forest, Luna and Pablo's steps are heavy but purposeful. The smooth black stone rests in Luna's hands, its faint warmth a constant reminder of what they faced and of what they have become.

The house looks smaller, its weathered wood blending into the landscape like it has always been a part of the mountain. The smoke curling from the chimney is comforting, a reminder that even in the midst of it all they have learned something.

Pablo sighs and runs a hand through his hair. "We are really doing this now, aren't we?" he said, his voice low but steady.

Luna's grip tightens on the stone. "We are. Together."

Once inside, the warmth of the hearth wraps around them like an embrace. The Codex is on the table, its pages fluttering slightly in a breeze from an open window. The symbols and drawings that had once seemed so foreign now feel like an extension of themselves, a language they are beginning to understand.

Luna places the stone carefully on the table, its black surface gleaming in the firelight. Pablo stands beside her, his hand resting on his pendant.

"So, what now?" he says.

"We learn," Luna says, her voice firm. "We listen. And when the time comes, we act."

Pablo nods, though his expression is uncertain. "What if we mess up? What if we don't get it right?"

"Then we try again. The mountain did not choose us because we are perfect, Pablo. It chose us because it believes we can grow into what it needs."

He laughs and shakes his head. "You sound like Juana María."

Luna smiles, her heart aching at the memory of their grandmother. "Maybe that's a good thing."

They spend the morning in quiet work, poring over the Codex and sorting through Juana María's collection of herbs and tools. Each page, each object, seems to carry a reminder of the legacy she left behind.

As the sun climbs higher, they hear a knock on the door and Pablo moves to open it. A young woman stands at the threshold, her face pale with worry. She holds a bundle in her arms, a small child, no older than two, with flushed cheeks and a laboured breath.

"Please," the woman says, her voice trembling. "I heard that Juana María can help. My son, he is sick."

Luna steps forward, her heart pounding. The fear of failure rises in her chest but she pushes it down, remembering Juana María's steady voice.

"Come in," she says, as she gestures to the woman. "We will do what we can."

The woman hesitates, her gaze darting between Luna and Pablo. "You are her grandchildren?"

"Yes," Pablo says. "We are the ones who will do her work from now on."

As he speaks, Pablo seems to stand a little taller, his shoulders squaring. The woman nods, her trust tentative but steps inside all the same.

Luna carefully unwraps the bundle to reveal the sick child. His small chest rises and falls unevenly, and his skin is slick with sweat. Luna's mind races as she recalls the lessons of Juana María and turns to Pablo.

"Find the *guayaba* leaves," she says. "And heat some water. We will need a poultice."

Pablo's hands are steady as he works, a stark contrast to the hesitation he had shown before. Luna is focused on the child, her fingers brushing its fevered forehead as she whispers a quiet promise to herself.

"We are going to help you," she says softly. "I won't let you down."

The minutes stretch into an hour, Luna prepares the herbs and Pablo keeps the fire steady. The woman watches with a mixture of hope and fear, holding her hands in prayer. And when the poultice is ready, Luna applies it carefully, her movements slow and deliberate.

The child's breathing begins to even out, and the flush fades from his cheeks. Luna feels a wave of relief, and tears appear at the corners of her eyes.

"You did it," Pablo says quietly, his voice filled with awe.

"We did it," Luna corrects him as she meets his gaze. For the first time, she does not see doubt in his eyes, but belief in himself, and in what they can become.

The woman weeps as she cradles her now-resting child. "Thank you," she whispers. "Thank you both."

The siblings stand in silence and watch as she disappears down the path, the weight of what they have just done settling over them.

"You think she will tell people?" Pablo says.

"Probably," Luna says. "And when they come, we will help them."

A small smile appears on Pablo's face. "We are really doing this."

"We are," Luna says, her own smile growing. "Because that is who we are now."

The light from the fire casts a warm glow against the darkening forest. The mountain watches as they step inside, its voice quiet for now. But Luna and Pablo can feel it, the steady hum beneath their feet, a promise that their journey is only beginning. And this time, they are going to do it together.

# CHAPTER 14

The Next Whisper

The next day, the mountain is quiet, its dense forests and towering cliffs bathed in a golden glow. A soft breeze rustles the leaves, carrying with it the familiar scent of herbs and wildflowers. The little wooden house nestled in the clearing looks much the same as it did years ago, though the vines creeping along the walls have grown thicker, more intertwined, as if the mountain itself seeks to protect the home.

Luna works in the garden; her hands covered in soil as she inspects the new rows of plants she had sown earlier in the season. Her pendant hangs around her neck, its smooth surface glinting faintly in the sunlight. The air is peaceful but she can feel the mountain's steady hum beneath her feet, a subtle reminder that its watchful presence never wavers.

A sound breaks through the quiet, footsteps on the forest path. She turn and wipes her hands as Pablo appears. He is taller now and broader, but his familiar crooked grin is the same. In his arms, he carries a bundle of firewood which he sets down near the house.

"Did you hear?" he says, his tone light but expectant.

Luna raises an eyebrow. "Hear what?"

"We have visitors," he says. "There's a family coming up the trail. A woman and her daughter."

Luna is immediately worried. "What do they want?"

"Help," Pablo says simply. "The girl has been having strange dreams. The kind that don't feel like dreams at all."

A quiet understanding passes between them. "The mountain has been whispering to her."

"It looks like it," Pablo says, a faint smile tugging at his lips. "I guess it's time to show her that she is not imagining things."

Luna glances at the horizon where the sun casts long shadows through the trees. "Do you ever wonder why it chose us?" she says.

"Sometimes, but I think I have stopped needing any answers. Maybe it doesn't matter why. It just did."

"I think about Juana María sometimes," she says, her voice barely above a whisper. "What she would say if she could see us now."

"She would probably tell us to stop wasting our time talking and get to work," Pablo says with a smirk.

Luna laughs, the sound light and free. "You are probably right."

They look to the path as the footsteps grow louder. A woman appears first, her face lined with worry, and in her arms is a newborn child. Beside her, a girl of about ten years clings to her skirt, her wide eyes darting nervously between the trees and the house.

Luna steps forward, her smile warm but calm. "Welcome," she says. "You have come a long way."

The woman nods, her voice trembling. "They told us that you could help."

"We will try," Luna says gently. She can't help but notice that the girl is staring at her pendant. "Come inside and tell us everything."

Pablo holds the door open as the woman and her daughter step inside. The air is warm, the fire crackling softly in the hearth. The Codex sits on the table, its pages open to a drawing of a tree with deep, twisting roots.

As Luna and Pablo get to work, the hum of the mountain grows a little louder as if it's watching closely.

The mountain has work and is calling to them again. Its voice carries on the breeze, and Luna and Pablo listen closely. They know exactly what to do, and it's all because Juana María entrusted them with a legacy. They know without a doubt that they have learnt to sing the song of the mountain.

# PART TWO

# CHAPTER 15

A Decade of Healing

The early morning mist clings to the slopes of the mountain, softening the outlines of the forest that cradles a small village. Pablo kneels by a cluster of wild *yerba buena*, his fingers deftly plucking the freshest leaves. His movements are steady and practiced, as if he had been born with the knowledge of which plants heal and which ones harm. A small woven basket by his side is already full of herbs destined to soothe a fevered child in the village below.

"Pablo, hurry," Luna says, as she calls from the edge of the clearing, her tone impatient. She stands with her arms crossed; a shawl draped loosely around her shoulders to guard against the cool morning air. Her dark eyes, sharp and unyielding, scan the trees as if expecting the mountain to whisper another secret.

"I'm not rushing this," Pablo replies, glancing over his shoulder. "You can't rush the mountain."

Luna sighs but doesn't argue. She understands as well as he the importance of the work they do. A decade has passed since their grandmother, Juana María left, but her lessons remained etched into their lives. Each herb they gather, every salve they prepare is an act of reverence for the mountain that took them in when they had nothing else.

The siblings follow a descending path back to their home, the weight of their baskets lightened by the satisfaction of a morning's work well done. Their house, modest and built from wood weathered by years of storms sits on a ridge above the village, a sentinel between the human world and the untamed wilderness beyond. Smoke curls lazily from the chimneys down below, and the faint scent of boiling *malojillo* or lemon grass tea wafts through the air, a constant reminder of their shared purpose.

Luna set the baskets down on the porch and turn to Pablo and brushes a strand of hair out of her face. "That was the last of the herbs we need for Don Esteban. We can take them to him after the tea is ready."

Pablo nods, his expression thoughtful. "He will recover. The fever is strong, but the mountain will guide him back."

It's in these quiet moments when they work side by side, that Pablo and Luna feel most at peace. Yet, even as they speak, an unspoken tension lingers. The mountain, their ever-present guardian seems restless of late. The wind whispers through the trees in strange patterns, and animals that once approached without fear now linger at the edges of the forest, their movements hesitant.

Luna notices someone approaching from the trail below. Her body tenses, her hand instinctively brushes against the pouch of protective herbs tied to her belt.

"Someone's coming," she says.

Pablo straightens up and sees a man and a woman dressed in crisp, modern clothing that looks entirely out of place against the rugged backdrop of the mountain. The man carries a leather satchel, and the woman has a notebook tucked under her arm, her polished shoes scuffing awkwardly against the uneven trail.

"Buenos días," the man says, his voice carrying an air of practiced politeness. "We mean no harm. Are you Pablo and Luna?"

The siblings exchange a wary glance. Intruders are rare this far up the mountain, and those who do come often bring trouble.

"Who's asking?" Pablo replies, his tone firm but not unkind.

The man steps forward and holds up his hands as if to show that he is unarmed. "My name is Mateo and this is Clara. We are archaeologists from San Juan. We have heard stories about this mountain and we are hoping you might help us."

"Help you with what?" Luna says, her voice sharp, her eyes narrowing.

Mateo hesitates and glances at Clara before continuing. "There's a cavern deep in the mountain. It is said to hold crystals, rare ones, with unusual properties. We have heard rumours about the healers in this village who might know where it is."

The words hit like a stone dropping into still water. The cavern. The sacred heart of the mountain. Pablo and Luna's faces darken simultaneously, their thoughts racing. This is what Juana María had warned them about. The balance of the mountain must not be disturbed, she had said. Its secrets must remain hidden.

"There's no cavern," Pablo says quickly, his voice steady but cold. "The stories are just that, stories."

Clara steps forward, her eyes bright with curiosity. "But surely you have heard of it? We have done extensive research, and…"

"There's nothing for you here," Luna says, her voice firm, brooking no argument. "Turn back. The mountain does not welcome intruders."

Mateo's brow furrows, and for a moment, he looks as if he might protest. But something in Luna's gaze, sharp and unyielding like the edge of a blade makes him pause.

"We didn't mean to offend," Mateo says, though his tone is tinged with frustration. "Thank you for your time."

The two intruders retreat down the path, their polished shoes slipping on the loose stones. Pablo and Luna stand in silence, watching until they disappear into the forest.

"They'll be back," Luna says quietly, her voice heavy with certainty.

Pablo's jaw tightens. "Then we will be ready."

As the wind picks up, rustling the leaves in a low, mournful song, the mountain seems to echo his words.

# CHAPTER 16

Strangers at the Door

The morning sun has barely broken through the dense canopy when the knock comes. It's firm but hesitant, a sound foreign to the small wooden door of Pablo and Luna's home. Luna freezes mid-step, her hand hovering over a pot of simmering *yerba santa* or mountain balm tea. She casts a sharp glance at Pablo who is sorting dried herbs at the table.

"No one knocks like that here," she says under her breath.

Pablo stands, his broad shoulders tense. "Stay here," he says, his voice low but steady.

He moves to the door, his footsteps soft against the creaking floorboards, and opens it just enough to see who's on the other side. There they are again, the man and woman from San Juan. This time, they are cleaner, better prepared, their clothes exchanged for sturdier, practical attire that looks new and out of place in the rugged mountains. The man, Mateo, gives a tight smile, while Clara adjusts the strap of a canvas bag slung over her shoulder, her notebook clutched protectively to her chest.

"We hoped you might reconsider," Mateo says, his tone polite but persistent.

"What are you doing here?" Pablo say, his voice cold, his body blocking the doorway.

Luna appears behind him, her presence quiet but commanding, her sharp eyes assessing the pair, noting every detail, the fresh mud on their boots, the glint of something metallic in Mateo's satchel, the faint, lingering scent of sweat and urgency.

"We are sorry to intrude," Clara says quickly, her words tumbling out in a rush. "But this mountain, it's extraordinary. The stories, the energy here, it's like nothing we have ever encountered before. We think it could be…"

"Stop." Luna's voice cuts through Clara's rambling like a knife. "You have no idea what you are talking about."

Mateo's expression hardens. "With respect, we have done our research. The cavern we are looking for isn't just a myth. It's real and could hold artifacts, crystals, materials that could benefit everyone, not just this village."

"It's not yours to take," Pablo says, his voice low and steady, a warning wrapped in calm.

Clara steps forward, holding out her notebook as if it's a peace offering. "We are not here to destroy anything. We just want to study it, to learn. This could be a discovery that changes how people see…"

"Enough," Luna snaps, her eyes blazing. She steps past Pablo, her presence like a sudden storm. "The mountain is not yours to study. It is not yours to *understand*. If you try to take from it, you will pay the price."

Mateo bristles, his frustration finally breaking through his polite facade. "We are not here to hurt anyone. But this cavern could be the key to…"

"Leave now," Luna says, her voice dangerously calm. "Before you wake something which you cannot silence."

A long, tense silence follows. The wind has gone still, and even the birds seem to hold their breath. Mateo looks at Clara, his jaw tight. Clara hesitates as if she wants to say more, but the intensity in Luna's gaze stops her. With a reluctant nod, Mateo turns and walks back down the path. Clara lingers for a moment, her eyes on each of the siblings.

"You're making a mistake," she says softly before following Mateo.

The door closes with a heavy thud, and Pablo exhales. "They will be back."

"Of course they will," Luna says, her tone resigned but firm. She moves to the window, watching as the intruders disappear into the forest. "But next time, they won't ask for permission."

"We need to check the cavern," Pablo says.

"And if they find it..."

"They won't," he says, even though his voice lacks conviction. "The mountain won't let them."

Luna turns to face him, her expression grave. "The mountain won't stop at just warning them, Pablo. You know that."

He doesn't respond. He doesn't need to. Both of them know the power of the mountain. Juana María had warned them: the mountain is alive. It listens, it watches, and it protects itself in ways that humans cannot comprehend.

As the siblings prepare to head for the cavern, the forest around them seems to shift. The wind whispers through the trees, carrying a familiar voice, low, mournful, and heavy with warning. The mountain is awake. It knows what's coming and so do they.

# CHAPTER 17

### The Sacred Heart

The trail to the cavern is not one that anyone could easily find. It's a winding thread through dense jungle, hidden beneath layers of ferns and tangled vines, marked by subtle signs shown to them by Juana María. A broken branch here, a cluster of moss-covered stones there, clues meant only for those who belong.

Pablo moves ahead, his machete slicing through the overgrowth with sharp, deliberate swings. Behind him, Luna follows in silence, her eyes scanning the forest with an alertness born from years of vigilance. The air is thick with humidity, the scent of wet earth and blooming flowers mingling with something heavier, something ancient and electric that presses against their senses.

They don't speak. There is no need. Both siblings can feel it. The mountain is alive. As they get closer to the cavern, they can feel its pulse quickening. It is not just the rustle of leaves or the occasional call of a coquí, a small frog, it's something deeper. The forest itself seems to breathe, each step a reminder that they are not walking through the wilderness but the body of a living being.

The entrance to the cavern is hidden behind a curtain of vines, its dark maw blending seamlessly with the rock face. Pablo pushes the vines aside and reveals the jagged opening. A faint glow emanates from within, not bright enough to light the way but unmistakable in its presence. It is the light of the crystals, the heart of the mountain.

"Are you sure it's safe?" Luna says, her voice barely above a whisper.

"For us, yes," Pablo says, his hand resting on the hilt of the machete. "But we have to check. If they find this..."

He doesn't finish the sentence. He doesn't need to. The siblings step inside, the cool air of the cavern wrapping around them like a shroud. The faint glow intensifies, illuminating the crystalline formations that jut out from the walls and ceiling like frozen lightning. The crystals are pulsing faintly, as if they are alive, casting soft eerie effects over everything.

Luna places her hand over a cluster of crystals and closes her eyes. "They're agitated," she says, her voice trembling. "I can feel it."

"The mountain knows that they are coming," Pablo says.

The cavern amplifies their words, and in response, the crystals glow brighter for a moment and then dim again, their rhythm as even as a heartbeat

"We have to protect them," Luna says, as she turns to face her brother. "If they bring their tools, their machines..."

"I know," Pablo says, his voice heavy. "But what can we do? They won't listen to us. They think we are just simple villagers."

Luna's eyes darken. "They cannot be allowed to find it."

Pablo's expression is conflicted and he understands her desperation. Juana María's warnings echo in his mind: *The mountain protects itself, but it also tests its guardians. You must be strong enough to carry its will.*

A vibration rumbles through the cavern, subtle at first but grows stronger. The crystals flicker, their light flaring brighter than ever, illuminating the siblings in an unearthly glow, and then, the ground beneath them trembles.

"Pablo," Luna says, her voice laced with fear. "It's angry."

"It's not anger," Pablo says. "It is warning us."

The vibrations subside as quickly as they began, leaving the cavern in an uneasy silence. The siblings exchange a glance, their expressions a mixture of awe and dread. The mountain is speaking, and its message is unmistakable.

"It knows they will come," Luna says, her voice trembling but resolute. "And it won't wait for us to decide. If they find this place..."

"They won't leave," Pablo says, as he finishes her sentence.

They leave the cavern in silence followed by the eyes of unseen watchers. As they emerge into the forest, the sun is already beginning to set, casting long shadows across the mountain. The wind picks up, rustling the trees in low, mournful whispers.

"The mountain is awake," Luna says, as she glances back at the hidden entrance.

Pablo grips his machete tighter. "Whatever comes next, we will face it together."

The mountain answers with a low, distant rumble, as if to remind them that they are not alone and that it too is preparing for the storm to come.

# CHAPTER 18

An Uneasy Calm

The days pass in a tense, watchful silence. The mountain, usually a symphony of life, chirping coquí, rustling leaves, and the steady hum of insects feels unnaturally quiet. Pablo and Luna carry on with their routines but with a growing sense of unease, their every action is shadowed by the knowledge that something is coming.

Pablo is outside sharpening his machete with deliberate precision. The metallic scrape of stone against steel echoes through the still air, each stroke a ritual of preparation. His jaw is tight, his dark eyes scanning the treetops as though expecting the intruders to materialise at any moment.

"They haven't gone," Luna says from the porch. She sits cross-legged, grinding dried *guayacán* bark into a fine powder. "I can feel it and the mountain feels it."

Pablo's expression is grim. "I know. It's too quiet."

Luna's hands work with practiced efficiency, though her gaze is always on the forest. The air seems heavier, charged with something intangible but undeniable. The siblings don't need to say it aloud: the mountain is holding its breath.

That afternoon, as the sun begins its descent behind the peaks, a villager arrives with urgent news. Don Ramón, an old farmer whose fields border the lower slopes of the mountain has spotted the intruders, but this time, they are accompanied by others.

"And they have been unloading equipment from a truck and they are setting up camp," Don Ramón says, his weathered face lined with concern. "They also have digging tools. It's no good, I tell you. It's no good."

Luna's grip on the pestle tightens, her knuckles turning white. "They're looking for the cavern," she says.

Pablo forces himself to stay calm. "Did you see anything else?"

"No," Don Ramón replies, shaking his head. "But they are stubborn and will keep looking."

After he leaves, the siblings sit on the porch in silence, the weight of the situation pressing down on them like the humid air. The sun casts long shadows across the forest, and the wind begins to stir, carrying with it the faint rustle of distant trees.

"They will find it," Luna says as she breaks the silence. "If we don't stop them, they will find the cavern."

"And then what?" Pablo says, his voice tinged with frustration. "We can't fight them, Luna. There are too many of them."

"We don't have to fight them," she replies, her gaze hard. "The mountain will."

"Maybe it's already awake."

"It's awake, Pablo. You can feel it, and it is waiting for us to decide."

His thoughts are churning. Juana María's words echo in his mind: *The mountain is a guardian, but it is also a judge. If you call upon its power, you must be prepared for what it demands in return.*

As night falls, the siblings head for the forest where the intruders have set up camp. Luna packs her protective talisman, while Pablo sharpens his machete once again. Neither one of them speak, the gravity of their task renders words unnecessary.

The path through the forest is dark, the trees towering overhead like silent sentinels. The wind grows stronger as they descend, carrying whispers that seem to come from nowhere and everywhere at once. The pulse of the mountain is slow but deliberate.

When they reach the ridge overlooking the camp, they crouch in the shadows, watching. Lanterns flicker in the gathering darkness, casting an eerie glow over the scene. The intruders move purposefully, unpacking equipment and studying a large, hand-drawn map spread across a makeshift table. Their voices rise and fall, punctuated by the occasional clang of metal on rock.

"They're getting closer," Luna says.

Pablo's jaw is tight. "We can't let them find it."

Luna reaches into her pouch and withdraws a handful of crushed herbs and recites a prayer under her breath. The wind carries her words into the camp below. And almost immediately, the intruders start to shift uneasily and look over their shoulders as though they sense an unseen presence.

"The mountain is warning them," Luna says, her voice soft but firm. "But it won't stop there."

Pablo's fists are clenched. "And neither will we."

The siblings slip back into the forest, their footsteps silent against the soft earth. The mountain whispers and follows closely, its voice growing louder with every step. It is not waiting for them to act; it demands that they act.

# CHAPTER 19

The Return

Pablo and Luna are gathering bark from a *ceiba* tree in the forest when they hear a low, mechanical growl and the rumble of engines. It is alien and intrusive, and cuts through the stillness. Pablo freezes and turns in the direction of the sound, his dark eyes narrowing.

"They have started," he says, his voice tight with anger.

Luna is gathering herbs but the mountain has changed and is now agitated and restless. The forest seems to shudder in response, and the wind stirs the leaves in sharp, sudden bursts.

"They didn't listen," she said, her voice edged with frustration.

They make their way to the source of the noise, moving swiftly and silently through the dense undergrowth. The closer they get, the louder the engines become, mingled with voices and shouted instructions and the occasional clang of metal. Luna's fists clench at her sides. It isn't just Mateo and Clara anymore. There are more of them now.

As they reach the ridge overlooking the camp, the scene below comes into view. The intruders have brought reinforcements, a team of workers with shovels, picks, and crates of equipment. A large tent has been set up, and trucks are parked haphazardly at the edge of the clearing. The workers move around with purpose, oblivious to the unease that hangs in the air.

"They've got machines," Luna says, her voice trembling with a mix of fear and fury. "They're serious this time."

Pablo's jaw tightens. "They will destroy everything if they find the cavern."

Below, Mateo stands at the centre of the clearing, gesturing at a map spread across the makeshift table. Clara is beside him, pointing at the forest as she speaks to a group of men with tools. Pablo and Luna watch as they began to fan out, their steps heavy and careless.

"They can't feel it," she says, her voice low. "The mountain is warning them, and they don't even notice."

The wind is picking up, bending the branches in unnatural ways, as if the mountain itself strains against their presence. The whispers grow louder, weaving through the air like an unspoken language that only Pablo and Luna can hear.

"We have to do something," Luna says, her voice firm. "We can't just stand here."

"If we interfere, they will know and it could make things worse."

"And if we don't?" Luna shot back, her eyes flashing. "They will find the cavern, Pablo. They will take everything and they will ruin it."

The wind surges and sends a cascade of leaves tumbling down from the treetops. It isn't just the mountain whispering anymore. The air itself is alive, charged with an energy that crackles against their skin. Pablo closes his eyes for a moment, listening, not to the intruders, but to the mountain.

"It's not waiting for us," he says, his voice quiet but resolute. "The mountain has already decided."

As if on cue, a deep rumble shakes the ground beneath their feet. The intruders freeze, and the rumble grows louder, more insistent, and then the earth beneath one of the trucks gives way, and the vehicle lurches sideways and into a shallow sinkhole. Shouts erupt as the workers scramble to pull it back onto stable ground.

"They think it's just the terrain," Luna says bitterly, watching the chaos unfold. "They don't realize that it's a warning."

Another gust of wind sweeps through the clearing, stronger this time, upending the tent and sending papers scattering into the air. Mateo yells something, his voice barely audible over the rising wind, but it's clear that he is trying to keep control. Clara grabs the map and pins it down with both hands as she shouts out instructions.

Luna turns to Pablo, her expression hard. "They won't stop, Pablo, not until they understand that this is no ordinary mountain."

He looks at her, his jaw set. "Then we will make them leave. Tonight."

That night, after the camp has gone quiet, they creep through the forest to the clearing. The moon hangs low in the sky, casting a pale light over the scene. The trucks are parked in a tight cluster and their tents are pitched nearby. A few lanterns are flickering, but most of the camp is dark.

"We will give them something to fear," Luna says, her voice barely audible.

Pablo reaches for the pouch at his belt. Inside are herbs and powders that Juana María taught them to use, ingredients that, when burned, can create a thick, acrid smoke. A symbol of the mountain's displeasure.

They work quickly and place the mixture in piles around the perimeter of the camp. As Pablo strikes a match and lights the first pile, the smoke begins to rise, twisting and curling in the moonlight like ghostly tendrils.

The wind carries the smoke into the camp, weaving through the tents and trucks. Within moments, shouts begin to ring out as the workers stumble around, coughing and choking. The smoke seems alive, and clings to them but refuses to disperse no matter how hard they try.

From the shadows, Pablo and Luna watch as the panic spreads. The whispering voice of the mountain grows louder, carried on the wind, its eerie cadence sends shivers down the spines of the siblings. The fear of the intruders is palpable as their voices rise in confusion and alarm.

"It's working," Luna says, her eyes fixed on the scene below.

Even as they watch, a sudden chill ripples up their spines. The whispers have changed, its tone shifts from a warning to something darker. The mountain is not satisfied with fear. It wants something more.

"Luna," Pablo says, his voice tight with urgency. "We have to go, now."

Luna hesitates, her gaze still locked on the camp. Then the ground begins to tremble and they take off and race through the forest. The mountain will finish what it has started.

# CHAPTER 20

The Mountain Stirs

The first sign comes with the dawn. Luna is preparing herbs in the kitchen when the tremor begins. It's faint at first, no more than a shudder beneath her feet, but it's ominous. She pauses, places the pestle to the side and listens. The mountain is stirring and she can hear its voice in her mind like the distant roll of thunder.

"Pablo" she cries, urgency sharpening her voice.

Her brother appears in the doorway, his face shadowed with fatigue from their midnight visit to the camp. He looks at her, then down at the floorboards, which creak and groan with the movement.

"It's starting," Luna says, her voice tight.

Pablo races outside and everything is unnaturally still, the symphony of birds and the that of the croaking coquí is absent, and even the trees seem to be frozen. The whispers are much louder now, a low, guttural sound that vibrates through the air.

"The mountain is angry," he says.

Luna wraps her shawl around her shoulders as if to shield herself from the weight of its fury. "They didn't leave," she says, her voice bitter. "They won't leave. They think they're safe."

"Not for long," Pablo replies grimly. "The mountain has lost its patience."

By midmorning, chaos erupts in the camp. From their vantage point above the clearing, they watch as the workers scramble to salvage their operation. The ground beneath the camp shifts again and cracks appear in the earth, faint but unmistakable. Equipment teeters precariously, one of the tents has collapsed, its stakes pulled loose as if by invisible hands.

Mateo barks out orders, his voice rising over the din. Clara hovers nearby, her face pale but resolute. Workers move with increasing desperation, hauling crates and tools as if trying to outrun the mounting sense of doom.

"They still don't understand," Luna says, her voice low. "They think they can control this."

Pablo's gaze darkens. "The mountain won't let them."

As if to punctuate his words, a low rumble echoes through the forest. The ground trembles and sends ripples through the clearing. A pile of tools clatter to the ground, and one of the workers stumbles and curses loudly. The workers exchange uneasy glances, their confidence eroding with each passing tremor.

"Pablo, look," Luna cries, her voice sharp.

At the edge of the camp, the forest is writhing and the trees are swaying unnaturally, their branches creaking as if pushed by an unseen force. Shadows move between the trunks, shapes that are not human but visible even in the daylight.

"They're coming," Luna says, her voice trembling.

Juana María told them stories about the guardians of the mountain, spirits of the forest, ancient and powerful who are called forth when the mountain is under threat. The shadows grow more distinct, taking on forms that are neither solid nor ethereal, their presence palpable even from a distance.

One of the workers sees them first and his face turns pale with fear. The trees groan and a gust of wind tears through the clearing, scattering everything like debris. The whispering sounds are almost deafening, its tone shifting from warning to fury.

Mateo steps forward and raises his hand as if to calm his men. "It's just the wind," he says. "Stay focused."

But his voice falters when the shadow guardians emerge from the forest, their forms indistinct but menacing. The workers back away and some drop their tools and head for the trucks. Clara stands frozen, her eyes wide and focused on the shadowy figures.

"They will run," Luna says, her tone firm but tinged with hope. "And they will leave."

"Not all of them," Pablo replies.

"They think they are stronger than the mountain," Luna says. "They are fools."

The ground trembles again, only this time it's worse. A crack splits the earth near the edge of the camp, and Mateo stumbles but doesn't fall, his jaw tightening as he grabs onto Clara's arm.

"We can't leave now," he cries.

Clara is not so sure; her fear is at war with her ambition.

"They won't stop," Pablo says, his voice heavy. "We will have to make it happen."

"If we don't, they will tear it apart."

The mountain demands action, and as the tremors grow stronger and the shadows of the guardians close in, Pablo and

Luna feel the will of the mountain settle over them like a mantle.

The mountain isn't just stirring anymore. It's awake and it's angry, and Pablo and Luna, its chosen guardians have no choice but to act.

# CHAPTER 21

The Call of the Guardians

They can feel its pulse beneath their feet, vibrating through the earth like a heartbeat growing louder with each passing second. The forest seems to lean in closer, its branches whispering in a language older than time. The mountain is calling them to act.

Pablo stands at the edge of the clearing, gazing down at the camp below. It's a scene of chaos as the ground beneath them buckles and cracks, workers scurry like ants, some drive away on trucks, while others try to salvage their equipment. The air is thick with tension, charged like the moment before a storm.

"They are going to see it through," Luna says, her voice tight with frustration. "No matter what the mountain does, they won't stop."

"Then it's up to us," Pablo says, his voice steady.

The mountain whispers and not just in the wind but in their very bones. It's more than sound, it's a presence, ancient and immense that demands action.

"You can feel it, can't you?" Luna says, her voice trembling. She looks at her brother, his expression both fearful and resolute. "It's in us now."

Pablo doesn't need to answer. The power of the mountain has been simmering inside of them for days, rising like water in a dam. It's not just a connection anymore, it's a force, raw and untamed, waiting to be unleashed.

The siblings descend into the forest, their movements silent and purposeful. Every step is guided, as if the mountain itself is showing them the way. The air grows heavier as they approach the edge of the camp. The whispers grow louder, filling their ears with words they can't understand but feel deep in their souls.

They stop just outside the clearing, hidden by the dense undergrowth. Pablo's breath is steady, but his hands tremble as he reaches for the pouch at his belt. Inside are the herbs and powders that Juana María taught them to use, tools for summoning the mountain's will. Luna kneels beside him and removes her own pouch and whispers a quiet prayer beneath her breath.

"Are you ready?" she says, her voice barely audible over the hum.

"No," Pablo says, his eyes fixed on the intruders. "But we don't have a choice."

Mateo and Clara are arguing and Clara's voice is sharp and tinged with panic, but Mateo is determined and unyielding. The workers have all but abandoned the campsite, scattering through the forest in a frenzy of fear. Only a few linger by the trucks, their faces pale, not knowing where to run as they watch the ground shift and crack.

"We're so close," Mateo cries, as he slams his fist on the makeshift table. "We can't just walk away."

"This isn't normal, Mateo," Clara says, gesturing toward the forest. "You have seen those shadow things. You have felt the ground move. This isn't just a tremor, it's something else."

Before he can respond, the ground trembles violently, a deep, guttural sound that reverberates through the clearing and silences them both. The trees at the edge of the forest sway as if pushed by invisible hands, their branches creaking ominously, and then the shadows become visible.

The remaining workers gasp and stumble, their eyes wide with terror. The shadows move like living things, their forms neither solid nor ethereal, circling the clearing, their presence is suffocating and oppressive.

"What are those things?" Clara cries.

Mateo doesn't answer. His face is pale, his jaw tight as he takes a step back, his confidence visibly shaken.

Pablo and Luna watch from a distance, their breaths shallow. The whispers have become a roar, a power that surges through them like a flood. The siblings can feel it in their veins, hot and insistent, pushing them into action.

"It's time," Luna says, her voice trembling but resolute.

Pablo strikes a match and lights the first pile of herbs. The flames crackle, and send a thick, acrid smoke spiralling into the air. Luna follows suit, lighting her own pile. The smoke rises quickly, carried by the wind into the clearing.

The effect is immediate. The intruders cough and stumble, their movements frantic as they are enveloped by the smoke, but this is not ordinary smoke, it clings to them, heavy and unrelenting, its scent sharp and otherworldly.

Mateo shouts something but his voice is lost in the chaos. Clara drops her notebook, her hands clutching at her throat as the smoke presses against her. The shadows move closer, circling the intruders like a predator stalking its prey.

Luna steps forward, her voice cutting through the din. "Leave here now," she cries, her tone commanding, her voice carrying the weight of the mountain. "Leave this place, or the mountain will consume you."

The intruders freeze, their eyes wide as they turn towards the siblings. For a moment, the clearing is silent, save for the crackling of the flames and the whispering wind. Then the ground trembles again, worse than before, and a crack splits the earth near the centre of the clearing, and debris flies around all over the place.

Mateo stumbles backwards, his face pale. "Clara, we have to go," he cries, his voice shaking. "Now."

Clara hesitates, her gaze darting between the siblings and the cavern they seek, but the ground gives another violent shudder and her resolve breaks. She grabs Mateo's arm and they turn and run.

The workers follow along behind, their shouts mingling with the roar of engines as the trucks tear through the forest path. The smoke lingers, swirling like a living thing, as the clearing falls silent once more.

Pablo and Luna, their breaths ragged tremble with what they have done. The whispers and fury has subsided, but the power of the mountain still courses through their bodies, leaving them shaken.

"They're gone," Luna says, her voice still unsteady.

"For now," Pablo replies, his gaze fixed on the lights of the retreating trucks. "But they'll be back."

Luna's expression hardens. "Next time, we won't just warn them."

"Next time, the mountain won't give them a choice."

As the first light of dawn breaks through the trees, the mountain seems to sigh, its presence settling into a tense, uneasy calm. But Pablo and Luna know that it's only a reprieve. The intruders felt the power of the mountain but they didn't yet understand what it was. The mountain is patient but not when it comes to its own safety.

# CHAPTER 22

Descent into the Cavern

The intruders return a few days later, and from their hidden vantage point above the forest, Pablo and Luna watch in grim silence as Mateo, Clara, and a handful of workers head for the heart of the mountain. Their steps are deliberate and their faces hardened with resolve. They carry picks, shovels, and lanterns, the weight of their equipment mirrored by the heavy determination in their eyes.

"They know where it is," Luna says, her voice tight with dread.

Pablo clenches his jaw. "If they reach the cavern."

"They won't," Luna says, her gaze hard. "We won't let them."

The entrance to the cavern is hidden behind a curtain of dense vines, but Mateo has a map, and his eyes scan the landscape with focused precision. Clara follows closely, clutching her notebook like a talisman, while the workers trail behind, their movements less certain. The events of the previous days has left its mark, the shadows, the smoke, the trembling earth, but this is a job and they cannot turn back now.

The air grows heavier as they get closer to the entrance, the forest falling unnaturally silent. Mateo pushes the vines aside and eventually finds the jagged mouth of the cavern where a faint glow emanates from within casting eerie shadows over their faces.

"This is it," Mateo says, his voice barely above a whisper.

"It's beautiful," Clara says, her voice tinged with awe. "We'll be the first to..."

A low rumble cuts her off. It's not loud, more like a growl from deep within the earth but it's enough to make the workers uneasy, their grip tightening on their tools. Mateo ignores them and steps through the mouth of the cavern.

"They have crossed the threshold," Luna says, her voice hollow. "The mountain knows."

"Then we go in after them," Pablo says.

"Once we're in there, there's no going back."

"I know," Pablo says, his voice steady despite the weight of her words. "But this is what we are meant for."

With a deep breath, the siblings follow Mateo and his gang into the shadowy depths.

Inside, the air is cooler, damp with the scent of earth and stone. The faint glow of the crystals illuminates the narrow passageway, their light pulsing like a heartbeat. Mateo's lantern flickers, its beam dancing over the jagged walls as they move deeper into the mountain.

Clara eyes are wide with wonder. "These caverns are incredible. They're almost alive."

"They're more than that," Luna whispers from the shadows, her voice low enough so that only Pablo can hear. "They *are* alive."

As they move deeper, the cavern widens into a vast chamber. Here, the crystals jut out from the walls like enormous spikes, their light like fractured rainbows. The air feels charged, thick with an energy that makes the hair on their arms stand on end. Mateo steps into the chamber, his lantern high, his eyes scanning the room with unrestrained excitement.

"This is it," he says, his voice echoing off the walls. "The heart of the mountain."

As his words fade, the cavern responds with a sound, a deep, resonant vibration that seems to come from everywhere and nowhere at once. The crystals pulse in unison and their light gets brighter and brighter.

The workers freeze, Clara's pencil slips from her grasp and clatters on the ground. "What's happening?" she says, her voice barely audible.

"The mountain is warning you," Luna says. "But you are too deaf to listen."

Mateo spins around, his face a mix of surprise and anger. "You," he cries, his voice breaking the tension. "What are you doing here?"

"Stopping you," Pablo replies, his voice steady. He steps into the light and Luna follows; her sharp gaze fixed on the intruders.

"You don't understand what you're doing," she says, her voice cold. "This place is sacred. If you disturb this place, the mountain will not forgive you."

Mateo scoffs, though his unease is evident. "Sacred? This is a discovery that could change the world. You're just scared of progress."

Clara steps forward, her expression no less resolute. "We are not here to destroy anything. We just want to study it, to understand."

"You don't understand," Luna snaps, her voice rising. "This isn't just a cavern. It's a living thing and it's listening, and it knows that you don't belong here."

Another rumble shakes the chamber, stronger this time. The crystals flare, their pulse quickening. The workers stagger and drop their tools as the vibrations intensify.

"We need to leave," one of them cries, his voice trembling. "This place isn't safe."

Mateo ignores him, his focus is locked on the siblings. "You think you can scare us off. This is bigger than you. And it's bigger than your superstitions."

"It's bigger than all of us," Pablo says. "And if you don't leave now, the mountain will make sure you never do."

A roaring sound reverberates through the caverns and the sound is deafening, a guttural cry that shakes the ground beneath their feet. Cracks spiderweb across the walls, and chunks of crystal fall from the ceiling, narrowly missing one of the workers.

THE CRYSTALS GET EVEN brighter, their light blinding, their pulse wild and erratic. The workers panic, abandon their tools and race down the passageway.

Clara grabs Mateo's arm, her voice frantic. "We have to go."

Mateo hesitates, his eyes darting between the siblings and the cavern, and finally, he agrees, and follows Clara to the exit.

Pablo and Luna are immobilised as the mountain's fury surges in time with their racing hearts.

"They won't come back," Pablo says, his voice quiet but resolute.

"They can't," Luna replies. "The mountain won't let them."

As the last of the intruders disappear into the passageway, the cavern calms down. The crystals grow dimmer, their pulse slows, and the rumbling subsides into a low, steady hum. Pablo and Luna stand in silence, their bodies still trembling in accord with the experience. The mountain chose them to be its voice.

# CHAPTER 23

The Wrath of the Mountain

The workers stumble down the rocky path, shouting frantically, their voices echoing through the forest, while Mateo and Clara follow along behind. Their trucks waiting at the edge of the clearing offer a promise of escape, but the mountain has other plans.

The ground trembles again, low and deep, as though the mountain itself has drawn a sharp breath. The forest shivers in response, leaves rustle and branches groan under the weight of an unseen force. The whispers that have been lingering in the air for days have been replaced by something darker, a guttural, growling presence that makes the air thick and heavy.

"They won't make it out," Luna says, her voice quiet but firm, her hands trembling as she clenches them into a tight fist.

They had warned the intruders and tried to stop them but now, the mountain has taken over. The first sign of its wrath comes as a sudden, violent crack. One of the trucks, parked too close to the edge of the clearing jolts as the ground beneath it gives way.

A gaping fissure opens up and swallows the front wheels and tips the vehicle forward. Workers shout in alarm and scramble to pull it back, but the truck groans and slides further into the chasm.

"Move, get away from it," Mateo cries as he waves his arms in an effort to save the terrified workers. His voice carries a desperate edge, and Clara is frozen, her wide eyes fixed on the fissure as it widens, inch by inch.

"It's the mountain," she cries, her voice trembling. "It's alive."

Mateo grabs her arm. "Snap out of it."

Another tremor shakes the ground, but this time, it isn't just the earth that responds. The trees around the clearing begin to sway, their branches creaking and snapping as if moved by an invisible force. Shadows dance between the trees, flickering and shifting in ways that defy logic.

"There's something in the trees," one of the workers cries.

The others turn, only to discover that the shadows have taken form as distorted figures with glowing eyes that flicker like embers. They move in closer, their steps silent, their presence suffocating. The air grows colder, the weight of the mountain's fury settling over the clearing like a heavy blanket.

"We have to do something," Luna says, her voice sharp with urgency. She turns to Pablo, her eyes wide.

"It's not ours to stop," Pablo says, his voice hollow. "The mountain has already decided."

The workers are scattering, some race into the forest, while others jump into the trucks. Mateo and Clara stand at the centre of the chaos, their faces pale and desperate.

"We can't just let them die," Luna says.

Pablo's expression is hard. "We warned them and they didn't listen."

The power of the mountain is surging around them, a wild, uncontrollable force that makes their skin prickle and their heart race.

"I don't want this," Luna says, her voice barely audible. "I didn't ask for any of this."

Neither of them had but the mountain doesn't care about what they want. They are the chosen ones, bound to its will, and now they are as much a part of its wrath as the shadows that stalk the clearing.

Another truck slides into a fissure, and the shadows move closer, their glowing eyes fixed on the remaining workers. One of the men drops to his knees, his hands clasped in prayer, while another bolts into the forest.

"Get to the trucks, now," Mateo cries as he grabs Clara's arm.

"It's too late," she cries. "Our tools?"

"Forget the tools, forget the cavern Clara, we just have to go."

The ground shakes violently again, and a massive tree at the edge of the clearing topples over, its roots torn from the earth. It crashes down with a deafening roar, cutting off the path to the forest and trapping the remaining workers. The shadows move closer, their forms shifting and flickering like living nightmares.

Mateo looks up and sees Pablo and Luna standing silently at the edge of the cavern, his face twisted with anger and desperation.

"You did this," he cries. "This is your doing."

"No," Pablo replies. "This is the work of the mountain and it is not finished yet."

The final blow comes as a roar, low and deep, that seems to rise from the very core of the earth. The ground splits open and sends a shockwave through the clearing that knocks Mateo and Clara off their feet and leaves them desperately close to a gaping fissure.

Pablo and Luna turn away. They don't want to see what happens next. The will of the mountain is absolute and its judgment is final. By the time that the tremors stop, the clearing is silent and the trucks are half-buried in the fractured earth and the workers are gone. Only Mateo and Clara remain, huddled together at the edge of the clearing, their faces pale and haunted.

"You were warned," Luna says. "The mountain does not forgive."

Mateo stares at her, his eyes wide with fear. "We will leave," he says, his voice trembling. "And we will never come back."

"We swear. Please, just let us go," Clara cries frantically, tears streaming down her face

The intruders have learned their lesson, but Pablo and Luna know that the fury of the mountain will never be forgotten. Its wrath has been unleashed and it will not be silenced.

# CHAPTER 24

Power and Sacrifice

The forest is still, eerily so, as Pablo and Luna make their way back from the cavern. The air is heavy with the remnants of the mountain's fury which lingers in the oppressive silence. Around them, the land bears the scars of the chaos: the earth has been fractured, trees have been uprooted, and a grey haze hangs over everything.

The mountain is quiet now, and its whispering voice is now but a low hum. It's anger has subsided, leaving behind a silence that is not peace, but something heavier, something else.

"They have finally gone," Luna says, her eyes showing signs of exhaustion. "Finally."

Pablo is staring into the distance watching as the last of the trucks disappear. His shoulders are tense, and his hands are still trembling from the power over which he had no control.

"It's not over and it never will be," he says. "The mountain is watching, but after today, it will always be watching."

"We did what we had to do,' Luna says. "Otherwise, they would have destroyed everything if we had not stopped them."

"Did we stop them, or did the mountain?" Pablo says. "Do you even know where we end and it begins?"

The question lingers between them as they make their way back to the village. The path is uneven, the ground scarred by the mountain's upheaval. The weight of their actions hang heavy on their shoulders, each step a reminder of the price they paid.

"I felt it, Pablo, when the mountain acted, I felt as if I was the one splitting the earth in two."

"I felt it too, and it's not just the mountain anymore, Luna. It's us and it's inside of us."

"Do you think it's changing us?"

"I don't think it is," Pablo says. "I know."

Back home, the siblings sit in silence. Their little wooden house, which once felt like a sanctuary, feels different now, as if the essence of the mountain inhabits the very walls. Their purpose, the healings, the quiet rituals of their lives feel distant now, like a memory from another time.

"We are supposed to protect this place," she says. "Not become its weapons."

Pablo sits across from her, his head in his hands. "Juana María warned us," he said. "She told us the power of the mountain would change us if we let it. I didn't understand then, but now I do."

"So what do we do? Walk away? Pretend we don't feel it every time the mountain stirs?"

He looks up at her, his eyes tired but resolute. "We keep going. We protect this place, but we cannot let it consume us."

"How?" Luna says, her voice rising. "You felt what I felt. That power is not something you can just ignore. It takes over, Pablo."

"And we have to let it," Pablo says. "Because if we don't, no one else will."

That night, the mountain speaks to them again, but not in whispers but in dreams, visions behind closed eyes, vivid and unrelenting. Pablo saw himself standing at the edge of a great chasm, the earth splitting beneath his feet. He felt the power surge through him, unstoppable and terrifying, and knew he had been the cause of it.

Luna dreamt of the shadows; their glowing eyes fixed on her as they circled closer. She reached out to stop them, only to realize that she was becoming one of them.

When they wake up the following morning, the house is cold, and the wind outside is howling. Luna sits up and looks across the room at Pablo.

"It's not done with us," she says, her voice trembling. "The mountain is still asking for more."

"Then we give it what it needs," he says.

Later that day, they return to the cavern and everything is much quieter now, the forest subdued but watchful. The hum grows louder as they approach, a rhythmic pulse that echoes their beating of their hearts.

They step into the chamber, their movements slow and reverent. The cavern is unchanged and the crystals are still glowing, but the air is heavier, charged with the weight and power of the mountain.

"We are its guardians," Luna says. "We don't have a choice."

Pablo looks at her, his expression softening. "We always have a choice, but it's not the one we want."

They kneel in front of the largest crystal, its surface smooth and cold under their hands. The mountain hums, its presence filling the chamber as if it wants them to know that they are a part of it.

The light reflected from the crystals is too overwhelming to resist and they allow it flow through them, binding them to the mountain in ways they cannot fully understand.

And when it's over, they are different, they are still human but now they really do belong to the mountain. It is calm now; its wrath has subsided and its will has been fulfilled. But as Pablo knows, this is only the beginning. The mountain has claimed them as its own, and their lives will never be theirs again. They are its guardians and they will always have to answer the call.

# CHAPTER 25

The Prophecy Fulfilled

The cavern is quiet but the air still buzzes with a power that they can feel in their bones. The mountain has settled down now, its fury has been spent, but the tension is heavy and unspoken.

Pablo breaks the silence, his voice low and strained. "It's done. The mountain is safe for now."

"For now isn't enough, Luna says. "What happens when someone else comes? What happens when it demands more from us?"

He doesn't answer, his gaze shifting to the enormous crystal at the heart of the cavern, its surface flickering faintly as if its alive. It had been glowing in rhythm with their hearts, but now it seems to be rest, as though it is satisfied with what has transpired.

"This is what Juana María warned us about," Luna says. "Not just the prophecy, but the mountain. She said it would it take everything if we let it."

"And now it has," Pablo says, his voice sharp. "And it's not just the mountain anymore, Luna. It's us. We are a part of it."

"We didn't ask for this, Pablo. We didn't choose this."

"No," he says. "But we are here and if we walk away now, who will protect it? Who will stop this from happening again?"

The prophecy had always been a shadow over their lives, but now it looms larger than ever, its truth undeniable. The mountain chose them, not just to heal, not just to protect, but to be its voice, its hands and its fury.

They step outside and the forest greets them with an eerie calm. The trees stand tall and still, their branches heavy with moisture from the morning mist. The ground, scarred by the mountain's wrath is quiet beneath their feet. It is as though the land itself is holding its breath, waiting to see what will come next.

"Can you feel that?" Luna says, her voice barely above a whisper.

Pablo felt it, the hum of the mountain, faint but ever-present, beating away in his chest as if it is a second heartbeat. It isn't just around them anymore; it's inside of them, an inescapable presence that binds them to the land in ways he cannot fully understand.

"The prophecy wasn't just about the mountain, was it Pablo? It was about us as well."

"What do you mean?"

"Juana María said the mountain would need guardians, but she didn't say why. Maybe it's not just about protecting it but what it makes us."

As they walk back toward the village, the weight of the prophecy on their minds, they moved in silence, their steps slow and deliberate. The forest is listening, its presence both comforting and oppressive. For the first time, Pablo and Luna truly understand what it means to be part of the mountain.

At the edge of the village, the familiar figure of old Doña Rosa appears, her weathered face lined with worry. She carries a bundle of herbs in her hands, her movements hesitant as she approaches.

"¿Están bien?, are you okay?" she says, her voice trembling. "We heard the tremors, the ground was angry."

"We are fine," Pablo says. "And the mountain is calm now."

Doña Rosa studies them for a long moment, her eyes narrowing. "But you are not. I can see it in your eyes. The mountain has taken something from you, hasn't it?"

"And it has given us something in return," Luna says. "It is what we are meant for."

Doña Rosa nods, her expression unreadable. "Just remember, niños, the mountain does not give without taking. Be careful of what you let it take."

Her words linger long after she has gone. That night, as the siblings sit on the porch gazing out over the village everything is quiet. The stars above are bright, undisturbed by clouds, but the stillness carries a weight that neither can ignore.

"We are different now," Luna says, breaking the silence.

Pablo responds wearily. "We have always been different."

"The mountain has changed us Pablo and I don't think we can ever go back."

He doesn't answer immediately but looks out across at the mountain which looms in the distance. "Maybe we are not supposed to."

"But what if it asks for more? What if one day, it asks for everything?"

Pablo sighs, his shoulders heavy with exhaustion. "Then we give it."

Luna doesn't argue. Deep down, she knows that he is right. The prophecy has been fulfilled, but it's not an ending. It's a beginning, a burden they will carry for the rest of their lives. The song of the mountain is now flowing in their veins, and the siblings sit in silence, knowing that their destiny is no longer their own.

# CHAPTER 26

A Fragile Balance

For the first time in weeks, the mountain is quiet, and for Pablo and Luna, it's a relief. He is standing on a bridge looking out over the valley while Luna is cooling her feet in a stream that has a steady peaceful rhythm, a stark contrast to the chaotic events of the last week.

As they are pleased to see, everything is back to normal. It's early morning and the village is coming to life, smoke rises from the chimneys, and people are attending to the first chores of the days. It's as if nothing has changed, but everything has.

"They won't come back," Pablo says as he breaks the silence. His voice is steady, but there's an edge to it that wasn't there before.

"You don't know that," Luna replies. "People like that, they always come back. Maybe not them, but there will be others. They will hear the stories and the rumours and they will think the same."

"The mountain will stop them," Pablo says firmly.

"And what if it doesn't? What if it needs us to act again? Do you really want to feel that power again, Pablo, because I don't."

The truth is, he can feel it coursing through his veins and tugging at the edge of his consciousness. The power of the mountain has left him feeling raw and vulnerable, as if a piece of his soul has been stripped away and replaced by something he doesn't fully understand.

Later, as they passing through the village, the villagers greet them with warmth and respect, but there's something else in their eyes, something almost reverent. It's as though they can sense the change in Pablo and Luna, even if they are not aware of its source.

At the edge of the square, Doña Rosa approaches, and in her hands she holds a tightly woven basket.

"You have done it, haven't you?" she says. "What happened with the mountain is all because of you."

"We did what we had to," Luna replies.

"Juana María would be so proud of you, but the peace with the mountain is not permanent. It's a fragile thing and easily broken."

"We know," Pablo says.

Doña Rosa places a hand on his arm, her grip surprisingly firm. "You are its guardians now, niños, but don't let the mountain take all of you. There is a balance in all things, even in the mountain."

Her words linger as they return home. The house, nestled at the edge of the forest feels smaller somehow, its walls too close, the air too still. The herbs they gathered days before are still on the kitchen table, untouched, their colours having dulled with time.

Luna touches the brittle leaves, her thoughts, contemplative.

"We can't go back to this, can we?" she says.

Pablo leans against the door, his arms crossed. "What else is there?"

"I don't know but I don't want to lose more of myself to this mountain, not if I can help it."

That afternoon, they return to the cavern, and the forest is calm as they approach the heart of the mountain.

"We were meant for this," Pablo says.

"Were we?" Luna says. "Or did the mountain choose us because it had no one else?"

"Docs it matter?" he replies. "We are here, and we are the only ones who can keep it safe."

"It matters to me."

They stand in silence for a long time, the prophecy has been fulfilled but the consequences are far from over. They are bound to the mountain now, and there is nothing they can do about it. Pablo and Luna look back before they leave, and they both know one thing for certain, that the balance is fragile and it is theirs to protect.

# CHAPTER 27

# Epilogue

The Legacy of the Mountain

The years pass but the mountain never truly sleeps. Pablo and Luna grow older, their roles as guardians are woven into every thread of their lives. The village prospers under their quiet watch. The forest, once restless and brooding hums with contentment. But the mountain never stops whispering. It's a low, constant presence, a pulse beneath the earth, a reminder of the power they carry and the price they have paid.

One cool evening with the moon high above the peaks, Luna stands on the porch, her shawl wrapped tightly around her shoulders. The wind carries the familiar scent of wild herbs and damp soil, the mountain's way of greeting.

Pablo appears with a carved wooden staff in his hand and leans against the railing, his face weathered by time and responsibility. They are older now, but the mountain has marked them in ways that go beyond age. Their connection has grown deeper, and even though the weight of it never lessens, they have learned to live with it.

The next morning, they are in the village when a family from San Juan appears, weary from travel. The wife holds a small child in her arms, his face pale and drawn with sickness. The villagers watch closely, their expressions a mix of curiosity and reverence.

With his staff in hand, Pablo steps out to greet them. The husband greets them in return, his voice trembling as he speaks.

"Are you the healers, the ones who speak for the mountain?"

"We are," he says.

The wife steps forward, cradling the child in her arms. "Please," she begs him. "Our son, he is sick. We have tried everything, but nothing works. They said you could help."

Luna checks the boy's temperature, only to find that his skin is clammy and his breathing is shallow.

"We will do what we can," Pablo says. "Please follow us up to our house."

The parents sit at the kitchen table as Luna prepares a poultice, her hands moving with practiced precision. Pablo selects herbs from the shelf and whispers a quiet prayer to the mountain as he does so. The air is heavy with the scent of sage and *yerba buena*, time-honoured rituals that are as much a part of the healing as the medicines themselves.

As they work, the hum of the mountain grows stronger, gentle and deliberate. After applying the poultice to his chest for over an hour, the boy stirs and his shallow breath becomes deeper and steadier. The parents watch in silence, their eyes wide with hope.

By the time the sun dips below the horizon, the boy is sleeping soundly and his colour has returned. The mother weeps quietly, her gratitude spilling over in whispered thanks.

When the family leave the next morning, the father turn to them and says, "Thank you, I don't know how you did it but thank you."

Luna leans against the door, watching as the family disappears down the trail "It's starting again," she says.

"It never stops," Pablo says.

"Do you ever wonder what our lives would have been like if the mountain had chosen someone else?"

"Every day," Pablo says. "But it didn't. It chose us."

"And we chose to stay," Luna says, her tone resigned but resolute.

They stand there for a long time, watching as the forest sways gently in the breeze. Even though the mountain is quiet, it is always in the background of their minds. But they know better than to think it will last. The peace is always fleeting, the balance will always be fragile. As the wind carries the scent of wildflowers and moss, Luna turns to her brother and says, "We will keep it safe."

Pablo nods as his hand tightens around his staff. "We always have."

The mountain hums softly in agreement and wraps its invisible arms around them in a familiar embrace. The legacy of the mountain is theirs to carry and they will bear it until the end, but as to who will inherit that task after they have gone is something that is always on their mind.

THE END

# CHAPTER 28

THE GODS OF SPACE AND TIME
A series of fantasy fiction stories.
THE ETERNAL OPTIMIST
BOOK ONE

Unlike his brother who is cautious and irritable, Addric has a bit of a reputation. He not only believes in miracles, he believes in the impossible.

Their holiday plans are sabotaged from the first day and they barely survive one life threatening situation after another. The stakes are high, and they have to succeed. A card-carrying member of the dark side is out to get his revenge, but they can't allow that to happen. Addric rises to the challenge and shows what he is made of.

He proves to everyone that he is both brilliant, and audacious. Fearless is a rollercoaster ride through an inter-dimensional realm, a place where unusual things can happen.

A drama set in motion long, long ago is about to unfold. All they wanted was a boy's own holiday. They had no idea what sort of holiday they were in for.

This story was selected as a finalist in The 2020 Book Excellence Awards.

THE OCEAN OF INFINITE MYSTERY
BOOK TWO

ALLOW YOUR MIND TO roam further than it has ever done before, to the outer perimeter of Alpha Centauri. It is here you will find a galaxy called the Khavala, an inter-dimensional realm, where many worlds exist side-by-side, a world of strange beauty, hidden power, and wondrous mystery.

The Khavala is a self-conscious entity, but when danger threatens the most sacrosanct of all domains, she calls upon the assistance of her most powerful creations, an invincible task force that includes Yumi Masters, and Warrior Angels.

To resolve this problem, they must travel deep into the heart centre of the Khavala, to a place of legend, to the domain known since time immemorial as The Ocean of Infinite Mystery.

## THE LAST DAYS OF LEMURIA
## BOOK THREE

Elisabeth Trundle's life changes on the day that she meets two attractive young men in The Great Library of London, but these guys are not Earthlings as she eventually finds out.

Elisabeth has been having dreams about the lost continent of Lemuria, but the last thing she expected is that she would actually get an opportunity to go there. And that would never have happened if the chronometer of a passing spaceship had not malfunctioned.

Accompanied by four Yumi Masters, Elisabeth's dream comes true, and she ends up in a civilisation that is about to be destroyed by a natural catastrophe.

Over the next two weeks, they have to train an army, defeat the high priest at his own game and save a young boy's life.

But it's not all bad news, the people are wonderful, and the food is even better. Before the dreaded day dawns, they discover how the Lemurians intend to survive.

THE GOLDEN PHOENIX
BOOK FOUR

Accompanied by a few feisty friends, Addric embarks on a mission to rescue his brother's girlfriend from the clutches of a necromancer with delusions of grandeur.

To save Elisabeth, they will have to battle it out in the Roman arena, cross the Arctic Ocean on a crystal powered boat, venture deep into the bowels of the Earth, and then brave the fires of hell on a volcanic planet on the verge of a major transformation.

It will take something more than sharp claws and attitude to defeat a necromancer at his own game, but these boys are Yumi Masters, and they have a few tricks up their sleeve.

## SAYONARA PLANET EARTH
## BOOK FIVE

The people of Earth have become obsessed with electronic devices, but if they want to survive, they have to make the biggest sacrifice of all. The big guys upstairs are willing to give them one more chance, but only if they change their ways.

Yumi Master, Addric Sharano, has been assigned the task of dragging them back from the brink. Unfortunately, there is a time limit on this deal. Addric spearheads a team of people who use every trick in the book.

Earthlings are about to find out that not all aliens have a bulbous head and big green eyes. Sit back and enjoy the ride as Addric reveals a few of his hidden talents.

## QUIETLY THEY CAME
### BOOK SIX

Yumi Master extraordinaire, Addric Sharano is back, and he is in fine form in this light-hearted adventure. Addric's new mission is to rescue forty-two orphans from Pompeii, before they are incinerated by the volcano.

Accompanied by his best friends and glamorous offsiders, Lady Felicity, and her sister, Countess Demetra, two exponents of the fine old art of subterfuge, and the modern version of sorcery, Addric comes up with a clever if not complicated plan.

However, there is one little catch. These kids have a greater purpose in life. They were born with a coded message in their DNA, and it is just waiting for an opportunity to be expressed.

Addric is not known as the master of spin for nothing, so, he takes the kids by the hands, and they dive into the deep end. And when they come up for air, they hit the big time.

Addric is the man with golden touch when it comes to doing the impossible, and he doesn't fail to deliver the goods in this rollicking romp of a story. Sit back and enjoy a ride that starts in Pompeii and ends on some of the great stages of the modern world.

## TEACH ME HOW TO FLY
## BOOK SEVEN

The future of an inconspicuous village is threatened by an ungodly invader, but a prophecy states that a messiah will come to their rescue.

The first person on the scene is a Yumi Master with a history of battling the bad guys. And not long after, the real messiah appears in a blaze of glory.

Disposing of the invaders is a serious business, but they have quite a few tricks up their sleeve, and the most potent weapon in their armoury is the power of sound. And when they are not doing that, they entertain the musically inclined villagers with a selection of inspirational songs from the 20th century.

# OTHER BOOKS

## A PRAYER FOR BROTHER WILLIAM

After he loses his parents, William Cahill, retreats into a world of his own and his life would have spiralled out of control if it had not been for Aunt Augusta. She drags him back from the brink and transforms his life and that of his siblings, but Augusta Cahill is no ordinary woman.

She might be dreadfully wealthy and a pathetic old socialite, but she can be a force to be reckoned with. A story about life, death and suffering on the home front, a place that can be as perilous as a battlefield.

This novel, which is both historical fiction and a romance is also a tender portrayal of love in some of its myriad forms. It was inspired by an old family legend and is a story that breathes life into a bygone era with vivid authenticity.

THE SNAKE CHARMER'S TALE
Also published as
KASHMIRA:
THE SNAKE CHARMER'S WIFE

An enchanting tale set in 19th century Ceylon and 21st century Australia. A shipwreck off the coast of Ceylon. A diary that hold a key to a long-lost treasure. A tale that spans two continent and two centuries.

After discovering a diary written by a snake charmer called Roshan in 1884, Jasper Powell finds himself in the middle of an age old mystery.

As he unravels the story, Jasper uncovers a key to a treasure that has been stored away in an inconspicuous inner-city Melbourne building for over one hundred years.

Jasper realises that he has a treasure of cultural and historical significance on his hands and decides to make Roshan's dream a reality.

A tale that is rich with vivid characters and exotic lands, The Snake Charmer's Tale is a journey of natural and supernatural delights, interwoven with holy men, magic and miracles.

As one reader has said, this story is 'Simply Amazing.'

## THE GODDESS OF GOOD FORTUNE
The Sequel to The Snake Charmer's Tale

When she is offered the opportunity to dispose of a recalcitrant necromancer, the illustrious Lady Felicity Originalis jumps at the chance. Lady Felicity is not your everyday detective. In fact, she is not a detective at all. She is an exponent of the fine old art of subterfuge, and the modern version of sorcery.

Felicity uses every trick in the book to protect a 9th century Arabian knight from the clutches of an evil Vizier. Memphalut el Shakar is the quintessence of a self-obsessed despot with the sharp but beady eyes of a pack hound.

Old-fashioned methods of torture are never on the agenda for Lady Felicity. She prefers to use other much more subtle forms of persuasion.

## A TALE OF AN ARABIAN KNIGHT

In the fabled city of Aggrabad, nestled in the Rub al-Khali Desert, a tale of epic proportions unfolds. This lost city of the Bedouins, likened to the Atlantis of the Desert, is a masterpiece of glistening white limestone, a freshwater oasis, shrouded in mystery and romance.

At the heart of this story stands Hakim, the noble Captain of the Guards, who finds himself caught in a web of intrigue and sorcery woven by a tyrannical Sultan and the wicked Vizier, Memphalut al Shikari.

The Vizier, a practitioner of the dark arts rules through fear and cruelty, disposing of his enemies in the most horrific ways. Hakim and his fearless girlfriend, Zenobia must do everything in their power to make sure that the plans of this evil Vizier never come to pass.

## I WILL BE PRAYING
## FOR YOUR SOUL

This story follows the journey of a cruel, violent and troubled soul, Justin Valéry, a twelve-year-old boy who torments everyone including his sister Majella and his family. After a terrifying experience in a church in Madrid, Justin mysteriously disappears, and finds himself in an alternate reality. He meets a mysterious man who informs him that he must embark on a journey of atonement and redemption. Justin undergoes a series of strange and challenging experiences in equally challenging environments and is forced to confront the consequences of his actions.

## THE PASSIONFRUIT HOTEL

In a world where the culinary elite reign supreme, a tantalizing tale of revenge, betrayal, and supernatural intervention unfolds. At the heart of this delectable drama is Susannah Velasnikov, a Contessa whose life takes an unexpected turn when her good-for-nothing brothers meet an untimely demise. She reinvents herself with a new life as the proprietress of The Passionfruit Hotel, but things take a turn for the worst when she becomes embroiled in a web of shady dealings and ill-fated entanglements with the notorious Lord Alfred Chili Pepper.

## MASTERMINDS OF MISCHIEF

KARIM AND LUCIA ARE culinary ninjas, stealthy, cunning, and not to be messed with. They are the guardians of gastronomy, and Knights of the Kitchen.

The Culinary Cabal holds the fate of the gastronomic world in their hands, but they are about to cook up a storm, inspired by a treasure trove of ancient herbs and spices.

In the world of culinary espionage, one false move and they could find themselves in the soup. A battle in the trenches of gourmet warfare is about to begin, and they have a world to save, one recipe at a time, before the Cabal can turn it into a pre-packaged nightmare.

Saving the world, one recipe at a time. It's about freedom, it's about creativity, it's about saving the culinary world. Don't even think about a future where every meal is a microwave tragedy

## MERLIN'S SCHOOL
## FOR ASPIRING LIGHTWORKERS
## DESTINY CALLS

The lush rainforests of North Queensland is the stage for Merlin's School for Aspiring Lightworkers. A fantastical tale of magic, cosmic education, and the transformation of a group of teenagers into powerful lightworkers.

At the heart of the story is Marlin Martin, aka, Merlin, of great fame and acclaim, disguised as a 24-year-old man on a mission. This is a story that conveys a message of hope, transformation, and the power of individuals to create positive change, guided by the wisdom and magic of the legendary Merlin Ambrosius.

## MERLIN'S SCHHOL OF MAGIC AND MYSTERY
## THE SORCERER'S APPRENTICE

In a secluded valley deep in the mist-shrouded mountains, an ancient castle stands as a bastion of arcane knowledge and metaphysical mysteries. This is Merlin's School of Magic and Mystery, where the legendary sorcerer has gathered students from all over 6th century Britain.

Among the chosen few is Alistair Thorne, a bright-eyed youth from a small village who has always felt a deep connection to the unseen forces of the universe. His abilities set him apart from his peers, but they also attract Merlin's attention, thereby earning him a coveted place in the hallowed halls of the school.

Alistair crosses the threshold into a realm of wonders, and under Merlin's watchful eye, he and his enigmatic friends delve into the secrets of the cosmos and the primal energies that flow through all living things

This story is a whirlwind of ancient rituals, and mind-bending incantations, one in which Alistair is swept up into a deadly game that will test his courage and push him beyond the limits as a sorcerer's apprentice.

## THE THRILL OF THE UNKNOWN

In the summer of 2024, a struggling German publisher, Marianna Bekendorpe finds an ancient book in a bookstore in Paris that transports her into a 6th-century tale about a young magician called Alastair Thorne, a protégé of the famous mage, Merlin Ambrosius.

Accompanied by his five best friends, Alastair embarks on a journey to spread the word that magic is the birthright of all. Wherever they go, they inspire hope, and sometimes skepticism. This odyssey teaches them that true magic lies within.

This story, which has been lost for centuries, resurfaces in Marianna's hands. And with the assistance of a talented production team, she transforms this tale and republishes it as, "A Magical Mystery Tour."

Marianna's company desperately needs a best seller, and she is taking a big risk, and hoping that this wonderful tale finds its way into the hearts of a modern audience. And if it does, her publishing house will finally be a global success.

## FROZEN IN TIME

A story about the quest of a passionate Neapolitan woman who decides to rebuild Poggioreale, a mountain village that was destroyed by an earthquake in Sicily in 1968. She battles bureaucrats, and politicians, but Florentina Grasso is a woman on a mission, and she will not be stopped.

Poggioreggio has too many memories to be assigned to the dustbin of history. But Florentina has a secret, a treasure that has been hidden away for centuries. This is a project of the heart, and it is not long before it attracts the attention of a money hungry entrepreneur with his eyes on a fortune. He has no idea who he is up against.

## THE MIRACLE MAN

What's the difference between a genius and an eccentric oddball. Not much if your name is Bonchance Fontainebleau. Bonchance stumbles through life, leaving a trail of pandemonium wherever he goes. A tale of a goodhearted vagabond with a sense of the absurd who does everything wrong and for whom everything turns out right. Armed with nothing but unwavering confidence, Bonchance defies logic, embraces chaos, and somehow manages to turn every blunder into brilliance.

# Don't miss out!

Visit the website below and you can sign up to receive emails whenever VINCENT GILVARRY publishes a new book. There's no charge and no obligation.

https://books2read.com/r/B-A-XYCOC-XEQJF

BOOKS 2 READ

Connecting independent readers to independent writers.

Did you love *The Song of The Mountain*? Then you should read *I Will Be Praying For Your Soul*[1] by VINCENT GILVARRY!

[2]

The story follows the journey of a troubled soul, Justin Valéry, a twelve-year-old boy who torments everyone including his sister Majella and his family. After a terrifying experience in a church in Madrid, Justin mysteriously disappears, and finds himself in an alternate reality. He meets a mysterious man who informs him that he must embark on a journey of atonement and redemption. Justin undergoes a series of strange and challenging experiences in equally challenging environments and is forced to confront the consequences of his actions.

---

1. https://books2read.com/u/3GJRap

2. https://books2read.com/u/3GJRap

Read more at https://vgilvarry.blog/.

# Also by VINCENT GILVARRY

**Merlin's School for Aspiring Lightworkers**
Destiny Calls

**Merlin's School of Magic and Mystery**
The Thrill of The Unknown

**Standalone**
I Will Be Praying For Your Soul
Masterminds of Mischief
Fun and Games at The Passionfruit Hotel
Merlin's School of Magic and Mystery
Frozen in Time
The Miracle Man
The Song of The Mountain

Watch for more at https://vgilvarry.blog/.

# About the Author

Vincent Gilvarry is a writer from tropical North Queensland in Australia, a multifaceted author with a rich and vivid imagination.

With a foundation in the visual arts, his transition into the realm of literature was sparked by a life-changing situation that inspired him to embark on a literary career and an odyssey that has lasted for over 25 years.

He boasts an eclectic repertoire that highlights his versatility across various genres and his fantasy fiction books in particular are a testament to his unparalleled imagination and to his narrative prowess.

Read more at https://vgilvarry.blog/.

# About the Publisher

Vincent Gilvarry is a writer from tropical North Queensland in Australia, a multifaceted author with a rich and vivid imagination.

With a foundation in the visual arts, his transition into the realm of literature was sparked by a life-changing situation that inspired him to embark on a literary career and an odyssey that has lasted for over 25 years.

He boasts an eclectic repertoire that highlights his versatility across various genres and his fantasy fiction books in particular are a testament to his unparalleled imagination and to his narrative prowess.

Read more at https://vgilvarry.blog/.

www.ingramcontent.com/pod-product-compliance
Lightning Source LLC
Chambersburg PA
CBHW021407150726
47989CB00005B/2444